DAILY 3 CARD SPREAD

BODY – CARD ONE REPRESENTS YOUR EXTERNAL REALITY

MIND –CARD TWO REPRESENTS YOUR ATTITUDE, BELIEFS, AND QUALITY OF THINKING

SOUL – CARD THREE REPRESENTS QUALITY OF ENERGY, YOUR INTERNAL DIRECTION AND GUIDANCE FOR THE DAY

PURPORT- as appears or is stated to be true but not necessarily true.

DAILY 3 CARD SPREAD

BODY - CARD ONE REPRESENTS YOUR EXTERNAL REALITY

MIND -CARD TWO REPRESENTS YOUR ATTITUDE, BELIEFS, AND QUALITY OF THINKING

SOUL - CARD THREE REPRESENTS QUALITY OF ENERGY, YOUR INTERNAL DIRECTION AND GUIDANCE FOR THE DAY

PURPORT- as appears or is stated to be true but not necessarily true.

DAILY 3 CARD SPREAD

BODY – CARD ONE REPRESENTS YOUR EXTERNAL REALITY

MIND –CARD TWO REPRESENTS YOUR ATTITUDE, BELIEFS, AND QUALITY OF THINKING

SOUL – CARD THREE REPRESENTS QUALITY OF ENERGY, YOUR INTERNAL DIRECTION AND GUIDANCE FOR THE DAY

PURPORT- as appears or is stated to be true but not necessarily true.

DAILY 3 CARD SPREAD

BODY – CARD ONE REPRESENTS YOUR EXTERNAL REALITY

MIND –CARD TWO REPRESENTS YOUR ATTITUDE, BELIEFS, AND QUALITY OF THINKING

SOUL – CARD THREE REPRESENTS QUALITY OF ENERGY, YOUR INTERNAL DIRECTION AND GUIDANCE FOR THE DAY

PURPORT– as appears or is stated to be true but not necessarily true.

DAILY 3 CARD SPREAD

BODY – CARD ONE REPRESENTS YOUR EXTERNAL REALITY

MIND –CARD TWO REPRESENTS YOUR ATTITUDE, BELIEFS, AND QUALITY OF THINKING

SOUL – CARD THREE REPRESENTS QUALITY OF ENERGY, YOUR INTERNAL DIRECTION AND GUIDANCE FOR THE DAY

PURPORT– as appears or is stated to be true but not necessarily true.

DAILY 3 CARD SPREAD

BODY - CARD ONE REPRESENTS YOUR EXTERNAL REALITY

MIND -CARD TWO REPRESENTS YOUR ATTITUDE, BELIEFS, AND QUALITY OF THINKING

SOUL - CARD THREE REPRESENTS QUALITY OF ENERGY, YOUR INTERNAL DIRECTION AND GUIDANCE FOR THE DAY

PURPORT- as appears or is stated to be true but not necessarily true.

DAILY 3 CARD SPREAD

BODY – CARD ONE REPRESENTS YOUR EXTERNAL REALITY

MIND –CARD TWO REPRESENTS YOUR ATTITUDE, BELIEFS, AND QUALITY OF THINKING

SOUL – CARD THREE REPRESENTS QUALITY OF ENERGY, YOUR INTERNAL DIRECTION AND GUIDANCE FOR THE DAY

PURPORT- as appears or is stated to be true but not necessarily true.

DAILY 3 CARD SPREAD

BODY - CARD ONE REPRESENTS YOUR EXTERNAL REALITY

MIND -CARD TWO REPRESENTS YOUR ATTITUDE, BELIEFS, AND QUALITY OF THINKING

SOUL - CARD THREE REPRESENTS QUALITY OF ENERGY, YOUR INTERNAL DIRECTION AND GUIDANCE FOR THE DAY

PURPORT- as appears or is stated to be true but not necessarily true.

DAILY 3 CARD SPREAD

BODY - CARD ONE REPRESENTS YOUR EXTERNAL REALITY

MIND -CARD TWO REPRESENTS YOUR ATTITUDE, BELIEFS, AND QUALITY OF THINKING

SOUL - CARD THREE REPRESENTS QUALITY OF ENERGY, YOUR INTERNAL DIRECTION AND GUIDANCE FOR THE DAY

PURPORT- as appears or is stated to be true but not necessarily true.

DAILY 3 CARD SPREAD

BODY – CARD ONE REPRESENTS YOUR EXTERNAL REALITY

MIND –CARD TWO REPRESENTS YOUR ATTITUDE, BELIEFS, AND QUALITY OF THINKING

SOUL – CARD THREE REPRESENTS QUALITY OF ENERGY, YOUR INTERNAL DIRECTION AND GUIDANCE FOR THE DAY

PURPORT– as appears or is stated to be true but not necessarily true.

DAILY 3 CARD SPREAD

BODY - CARD ONE REPRESENTS YOUR EXTERNAL REALITY

MIND -CARD TWO REPRESENTS YOUR ATTITUDE, BELIEFS, AND QUALITY OF THINKING

SOUL - CARD THREE REPRESENTS QUALITY OF ENERGY, YOUR INTERNAL DIRECTION AND GUIDANCE FOR THE DAY

PURPORT- as appears or is stated to be true but not necessarily true.

DAILY 3 CARD SPREAD

BODY - CARD ONE REPRESENTS YOUR EXTERNAL REALITY

MIND -CARD TWO REPRESENTS YOUR ATTITUDE, BELIEFS, AND QUALITY OF THINKING

SOUL - CARD THREE REPRESENTS QUALITY OF ENERGY, YOUR INTERNAL DIRECTION AND GUIDANCE FOR THE DAY

PURPORT- as appears or is stated to be true but not necessarily true.

DAILY 3 CARD SPREAD

BODY – CARD ONE REPRESENTS YOUR EXTERNAL REALITY

MIND –CARD TWO REPRESENTS YOUR ATTITUDE, BELIEFS, AND QUALITY OF THINKING

SOUL – CARD THREE REPRESENTS QUALITY OF ENERGY, YOUR INTERNAL DIRECTION AND GUIDANCE FOR THE DAY

PURPORT– as appears or is stated to be true but not necessarily true.

DAILY 3 CARD SPREAD

BODY - CARD ONE REPRESENTS YOUR EXTERNAL REALITY

MIND -CARD TWO REPRESENTS YOUR ATTITUDE, BELIEFS, AND QUALITY OF THINKING

SOUL - CARD THREE REPRESENTS QUALITY OF ENERGY, YOUR INTERNAL DIRECTION AND GUIDANCE FOR THE DAY

PURPORT- as appears or is stated to be true but not necessarily true.

DAILY 3 CARD SPREAD

BODY – CARD ONE REPRESENTS YOUR EXTERNAL REALITY

MIND –CARD TWO REPRESENTS YOUR ATTITUDE, BELIEFS, AND QUALITY OF THINKING

SOUL – CARD THREE REPRESENTS QUALITY OF ENERGY, YOUR INTERNAL DIRECTION AND GUIDANCE FOR THE DAY

PURPORT– as appears or is stated to be true but not necessarily true.

DAILY 3 CARD SPREAD

BODY - CARD ONE REPRESENTS YOUR EXTERNAL REALITY

MIND -CARD TWO REPRESENTS YOUR ATTITUDE, BELIEFS, AND QUALITY OF THINKING

SOUL - CARD THREE REPRESENTS QUALITY OF ENERGY, YOUR INTERNAL DIRECTION AND GUIDANCE FOR THE DAY

PURPORT- as appears or is stated to be true but not necessarily true.

DAILY 3 CARD SPREAD

BODY – CARD ONE REPRESENTS YOUR EXTERNAL REALITY

MIND –CARD TWO REPRESENTS YOUR ATTITUDE, BELIEFS, AND QUALITY OF THINKING

SOUL – CARD THREE REPRESENTS QUALITY OF ENERGY, YOUR INTERNAL DIRECTION AND GUIDANCE FOR THE DAY

PURPORT– as appears or is stated to be true but not necessarily true.

DAILY 3 CARD SPREAD

BODY - CARD ONE REPRESENTS YOUR EXTERNAL REALITY

MIND -CARD TWO REPRESENTS YOUR ATTITUDE, BELIEFS, AND QUALITY OF THINKING

SOUL - CARD THREE REPRESENTS QUALITY OF ENERGY, YOUR INTERNAL DIRECTION AND GUIDANCE FOR THE DAY

PURPORT- as appears or is stated to be true but not necessarily true.

DAILY 3 CARD SPREAD

BODY - CARD ONE REPRESENTS YOUR EXTERNAL REALITY

MIND -CARD TWO REPRESENTS YOUR ATTITUDE, BELIEFS, AND QUALITY OF THINKING

SOUL - CARD THREE REPRESENTS QUALITY OF ENERGY, YOUR INTERNAL DIRECTION AND GUIDANCE FOR THE DAY

PURPORT- as appears or is stated to be true but not necessarily true.

DAILY 3 CARD SPREAD

BODY - CARD ONE REPRESENTS YOUR EXTERNAL REALITY

MIND -CARD TWO REPRESENTS YOUR ATTITUDE, BELIEFS, AND QUALITY OF THINKING

SOUL - CARD THREE REPRESENTS QUALITY OF ENERGY, YOUR INTERNAL DIRECTION AND GUIDANCE FOR THE DAY

PURPORT- as appears or is stated to be true but not necessarily true.

DAILY 3 CARD SPREAD

BODY – CARD ONE REPRESENTS YOUR EXTERNAL REALITY

MIND –CARD TWO REPRESENTS YOUR ATTITUDE, BELIEFS, AND QUALITY OF THINKING

SOUL – CARD THREE REPRESENTS QUALITY OF ENERGY, YOUR INTERNAL DIRECTION AND GUIDANCE FOR THE DAY

PURPORT– as appears or is stated to be true but not necessarily true.

DAILY 3 CARD SPREAD

BODY - CARD ONE REPRESENTS YOUR EXTERNAL REALITY

MIND -CARD TWO REPRESENTS YOUR ATTITUDE, BELIEFS, AND QUALITY OF THINKING

SOUL - CARD THREE REPRESENTS QUALITY OF ENERGY, YOUR INTERNAL DIRECTION AND GUIDANCE FOR THE DAY

PURPORT- as appears or is stated to be true but not necessarily true.

DAILY 3 CARD SPREAD

BODY - CARD ONE REPRESENTS YOUR EXTERNAL REALITY

MIND -CARD TWO REPRESENTS YOUR ATTITUDE, BELIEFS, AND QUALITY OF THINKING

SOUL - CARD THREE REPRESENTS QUALITY OF ENERGY, YOUR INTERNAL DIRECTION AND GUIDANCE FOR THE DAY

PURPORT- as appears or is stated to be true but not necessarily true.

DAILY 3 CARD SPREAD

BODY - CARD ONE REPRESENTS YOUR EXTERNAL REALITY

MIND -CARD TWO REPRESENTS YOUR ATTITUDE, BELIEFS, AND QUALITY OF THINKING

SOUL - CARD THREE REPRESENTS QUALITY OF ENERGY, YOUR INTERNAL DIRECTION AND GUIDANCE FOR THE DAY

PURPORT- as appears or is stated to be true but not necessarily true.

DAILY 3 CARD SPREAD

BODY - CARD ONE REPRESENTS YOUR EXTERNAL REALITY

MIND - CARD TWO REPRESENTS YOUR ATTITUDE, BELIEFS, AND QUALITY OF THINKING

SOUL - CARD THREE REPRESENTS QUALITY OF ENERGY, YOUR INTERNAL DIRECTION AND GUIDANCE FOR THE DAY

PURPORT- as appears or is stated to be true but not necessarily true.

DAILY 3 CARD SPREAD

BODY – CARD ONE REPRESENTS YOUR EXTERNAL REALITY

MIND –CARD TWO REPRESENTS YOUR ATTITUDE, BELIEFS, AND QUALITY OF THINKING

SOUL – CARD THREE REPRESENTS QUALITY OF ENERGY, YOUR INTERNAL DIRECTION AND GUIDANCE FOR THE DAY

PURPORT- as appears or is stated to be true but not necessarily true.

DAILY 3 CARD SPREAD

BODY - CARD ONE REPRESENTS YOUR EXTERNAL REALITY

MIND -CARD TWO REPRESENTS YOUR ATTITUDE, BELIEFS, AND QUALITY OF THINKING

SOUL - CARD THREE REPRESENTS QUALITY OF ENERGY, YOUR INTERNAL DIRECTION AND GUIDANCE FOR THE DAY

PURPORT- as appears or is stated to be true but not necessarily true.

DAILY 3 CARD SPREAD

BODY – CARD ONE REPRESENTS YOUR EXTERNAL REALITY

MIND –CARD TWO REPRESENTS YOUR ATTITUDE, BELIEFS, AND QUALITY OF THINKING

SOUL – CARD THREE REPRESENTS QUALITY OF ENERGY, YOUR INTERNAL DIRECTION AND GUIDANCE FOR THE DAY

PURPORT- as appears or is stated to be true but not necessarily true.

DAILY 3 CARD SPREAD

BODY - CARD ONE REPRESENTS YOUR EXTERNAL REALITY

MIND -CARD TWO REPRESENTS YOUR ATTITUDE, BELIEFS, AND QUALITY OF THINKING

SOUL - CARD THREE REPRESENTS QUALITY OF ENERGY, YOUR INTERNAL DIRECTION AND GUIDANCE FOR THE DAY

PURPORT- as appears or is stated to be true but not necessarily true.

DAILY 3 CARD SPREAD

BODY – CARD ONE REPRESENTS YOUR EXTERNAL REALITY

MIND –CARD TWO REPRESENTS YOUR ATTITUDE, BELIEFS, AND QUALITY OF THINKING

SOUL – CARD THREE REPRESENTS QUALITY OF ENERGY, YOUR INTERNAL DIRECTION AND GUIDANCE FOR THE DAY

PURPORT- as appears or is stated to be true but not necessarily true.

DAILY 3 CARD SPREAD

BODY - CARD ONE REPRESENTS YOUR EXTERNAL REALITY

MIND -CARD TWO REPRESENTS YOUR ATTITUDE, BELIEFS, AND QUALITY OF THINKING

SOUL - CARD THREE REPRESENTS QUALITY OF ENERGY, YOUR INTERNAL DIRECTION AND GUIDANCE FOR THE DAY

PURPORT- as appears or is stated to be true but not necessarily true.

DAILY 3 CARD SPREAD

BODY - CARD ONE REPRESENTS YOUR EXTERNAL REALITY

MIND -CARD TWO REPRESENTS YOUR ATTITUDE, BELIEFS, AND QUALITY OF THINKING

SOUL - CARD THREE REPRESENTS QUALITY OF ENERGY, YOUR INTERNAL DIRECTION AND GUIDANCE FOR THE DAY

PURPORT- as appears or is stated to be true but not necessarily true.

DAILY 3 CARD SPREAD

BODY - CARD ONE REPRESENTS YOUR EXTERNAL REALITY

MIND -CARD TWO REPRESENTS YOUR ATTITUDE, BELIEFS, AND QUALITY OF THINKING

SOUL - CARD THREE REPRESENTS QUALITY OF ENERGY, YOUR INTERNAL DIRECTION AND GUIDANCE FOR THE DAY

PURPORT- as appears or is stated to be true but not necessarily true.

DAILY 3 CARD SPREAD

BODY - CARD ONE REPRESENTS YOUR EXTERNAL REALITY

MIND -CARD TWO REPRESENTS YOUR ATTITUDE, BELIEFS, AND QUALITY OF THINKING

SOUL - CARD THREE REPRESENTS QUALITY OF ENERGY, YOUR INTERNAL DIRECTION AND GUIDANCE FOR THE DAY

PURPORT- as appears or is stated to be true but not necessarily true.

DAILY 3 CARD SPREAD

BODY – CARD ONE REPRESENTS YOUR EXTERNAL REALITY

MIND –CARD TWO REPRESENTS YOUR ATTITUDE, BELIEFS, AND QUALITY OF THINKING

SOUL – CARD THREE REPRESENTS QUALITY OF ENERGY, YOUR INTERNAL DIRECTION AND GUIDANCE FOR THE DAY

PURPORT– as appears or is stated to be true but not necessarily true.

DAILY 3 CARD SPREAD

BODY - CARD ONE REPRESENTS YOUR EXTERNAL REALITY

MIND -CARD TWO REPRESENTS YOUR ATTITUDE, BELIEFS, AND QUALITY OF THINKING

SOUL - CARD THREE REPRESENTS QUALITY OF ENERGY, YOUR INTERNAL DIRECTION AND GUIDANCE FOR THE DAY

PURPORT- as appears or is stated to be true but not necessarily true.

DAILY 3 CARD SPREAD

BODY – CARD ONE REPRESENTS YOUR EXTERNAL REALITY

MIND –CARD TWO REPRESENTS YOUR ATTITUDE, BELIEFS, AND QUALITY OF THINKING

SOUL – CARD THREE REPRESENTS QUALITY OF ENERGY, YOUR INTERNAL DIRECTION AND GUIDANCE FOR THE DAY

PURPORT– as appears or is stated to be true but not necessarily true.

DAILY 3 CARD SPREAD

BODY - CARD ONE REPRESENTS YOUR EXTERNAL REALITY

MIND -CARD TWO REPRESENTS YOUR ATTITUDE, BELIEFS, AND QUALITY OF THINKING

SOUL - CARD THREE REPRESENTS QUALITY OF ENERGY, YOUR INTERNAL DIRECTION AND GUIDANCE FOR THE DAY

PURPORT- as appears or is stated to be true but not necessarily true.

DAILY 3 CARD SPREAD

BODY – CARD ONE REPRESENTS YOUR EXTERNAL REALITY

MIND –CARD TWO REPRESENTS YOUR ATTITUDE, BELIEFS, AND QUALITY OF THINKING

SOUL – CARD THREE REPRESENTS QUALITY OF ENERGY, YOUR INTERNAL DIRECTION AND GUIDANCE FOR THE DAY

PURPORT– as appears or is stated to be true but not necessarily true.

DAILY 3 CARD SPREAD

BODY - CARD ONE REPRESENTS YOUR EXTERNAL REALITY

MIND -CARD TWO REPRESENTS YOUR ATTITUDE, BELIEFS, AND QUALITY OF THINKING

SOUL - CARD THREE REPRESENTS QUALITY OF ENERGY, YOUR INTERNAL DIRECTION AND GUIDANCE FOR THE DAY

PURPORT- as appears or is stated to be true but not necessarily true.

DAILY 3 CARD SPREAD

BODY - CARD ONE REPRESENTS YOUR EXTERNAL REALITY

MIND -CARD TWO REPRESENTS YOUR ATTITUDE, BELIEFS, AND QUALITY OF THINKING

SOUL - CARD THREE REPRESENTS QUALITY OF ENERGY, YOUR INTERNAL DIRECTION AND GUIDANCE FOR THE DAY

PURPORT- as appears or is stated to be true but not necessarily true.

DAILY 3 CARD SPREAD

BODY - CARD ONE REPRESENTS YOUR EXTERNAL REALITY

MIND -CARD TWO REPRESENTS YOUR ATTITUDE, BELIEFS, AND QUALITY OF THINKING

SOUL - CARD THREE REPRESENTS QUALITY OF ENERGY, YOUR INTERNAL DIRECTION AND GUIDANCE FOR THE DAY

PURPORT- as appears or is stated to be true but not necessarily true.

DAILY 3 CARD SPREAD

BODY – CARD ONE REPRESENTS YOUR EXTERNAL REALITY

MIND –CARD TWO REPRESENTS YOUR ATTITUDE, BELIEFS, AND QUALITY OF THINKING

SOUL – CARD THREE REPRESENTS QUALITY OF ENERGY, YOUR INTERNAL DIRECTION AND GUIDANCE FOR THE DAY

PURPORT– as appears or is stated to be true but not necessarily true.

DAILY 3 CARD SPREAD

BODY - CARD ONE REPRESENTS YOUR EXTERNAL REALITY

MIND -CARD TWO REPRESENTS YOUR ATTITUDE, BELIEFS, AND QUALITY OF THINKING

SOUL - CARD THREE REPRESENTS QUALITY OF ENERGY, YOUR INTERNAL DIRECTION AND GUIDANCE FOR THE DAY

PURPORT- as appears or is stated to be true but not necessarily true.

DAILY 3 CARD SPREAD

BODY – CARD ONE REPRESENTS YOUR EXTERNAL REALITY

MIND –CARD TWO REPRESENTS YOUR ATTITUDE, BELIEFS, AND QUALITY OF THINKING

SOUL – CARD THREE REPRESENTS QUALITY OF ENERGY, YOUR INTERNAL DIRECTION AND GUIDANCE FOR THE DAY

PURPORT– as appears or is stated to be true but not necessarily true.

DAILY 3 CARD SPREAD

BODY - CARD ONE REPRESENTS YOUR EXTERNAL REALITY

MIND -CARD TWO REPRESENTS YOUR ATTITUDE, BELIEFS, AND QUALITY OF THINKING

SOUL - CARD THREE REPRESENTS QUALITY OF ENERGY, YOUR INTERNAL DIRECTION AND GUIDANCE FOR THE DAY

PURPORT- as appears or is stated to be true but not necessarily true.

DAILY 3 CARD SPREAD

BODY - CARD ONE REPRESENTS YOUR EXTERNAL REALITY

MIND -CARD TWO REPRESENTS YOUR ATTITUDE, BELIEFS, AND QUALITY OF THINKING

SOUL - CARD THREE REPRESENTS QUALITY OF ENERGY, YOUR INTERNAL DIRECTION AND GUIDANCE FOR THE DAY

PURPORT- as appears or is stated to be true but not necessarily true.

DAILY 3 CARD SPREAD

BODY – CARD ONE REPRESENTS YOUR EXTERNAL REALITY

MIND –CARD TWO REPRESENTS YOUR ATTITUDE, BELIEFS, AND QUALITY OF THINKING

SOUL – CARD THREE REPRESENTS QUALITY OF ENERGY, YOUR INTERNAL DIRECTION AND GUIDANCE FOR THE DAY

PURPORT– as appears or is stated to be true but not necessarily true.

DAILY 3 CARD SPREAD

BODY - CARD ONE REPRESENTS YOUR EXTERNAL REALITY

MIND -CARD TWO REPRESENTS YOUR ATTITUDE, BELIEFS, AND QUALITY OF THINKING

SOUL - CARD THREE REPRESENTS QUALITY OF ENERGY, YOUR INTERNAL DIRECTION AND GUIDANCE FOR THE DAY

PURPORT- as appears or is stated to be true but not necessarily true.

DAILY 3 CARD SPREAD

BODY - CARD ONE REPRESENTS YOUR
EXTERNAL REALITY

MIND -CARD TWO REPRESENTS YOUR
ATTITUDE, BELIEFS, AND QUALITY OF
THINKING

SOUL - CARD THREE REPRESENTS
QUALITY OF ENERGY, YOUR INTERNAL
DIRECTION AND GUIDANCE FOR THE
DAY

PURPORT- as appears or is stated to be
true but not necessarily true.

DAILY 3 CARD SPREAD

BODY - CARD ONE REPRESENTS YOUR EXTERNAL REALITY

MIND -CARD TWO REPRESENTS YOUR ATTITUDE, BELIEFS, AND QUALITY OF THINKING

SOUL - CARD THREE REPRESENTS QUALITY OF ENERGY, YOUR INTERNAL DIRECTION AND GUIDANCE FOR THE DAY

PURPORT- as appears or is stated to be true but not necessarily true.

DAILY 3 CARD SPREAD

BODY - CARD ONE REPRESENTS YOUR EXTERNAL REALITY

MIND -CARD TWO REPRESENTS YOUR ATTITUDE, BELIEFS, AND QUALITY OF THINKING

SOUL - CARD THREE REPRESENTS QUALITY OF ENERGY, YOUR INTERNAL DIRECTION AND GUIDANCE FOR THE DAY

PURPORT- as appears or is stated to be true but not necessarily true.

DAILY 3 CARD SPREAD

BODY - CARD ONE REPRESENTS YOUR EXTERNAL REALITY

MIND -CARD TWO REPRESENTS YOUR ATTITUDE, BELIEFS, AND QUALITY OF THINKING

SOUL - CARD THREE REPRESENTS QUALITY OF ENERGY, YOUR INTERNAL DIRECTION AND GUIDANCE FOR THE DAY

PURPORT- as appears or is stated to be true but not necessarily true.

DAILY 3 CARD SPREAD

BODY – CARD ONE REPRESENTS YOUR EXTERNAL REALITY

MIND –CARD TWO REPRESENTS YOUR ATTITUDE, BELIEFS, AND QUALITY OF THINKING

SOUL – CARD THREE REPRESENTS QUALITY OF ENERGY, YOUR INTERNAL DIRECTION AND GUIDANCE FOR THE DAY

PURPORT- as appears or is stated to be true but not necessarily true.

DAILY 3 CARD SPREAD

BODY - CARD ONE REPRESENTS YOUR EXTERNAL REALITY

MIND -CARD TWO REPRESENTS YOUR ATTITUDE, BELIEFS, AND QUALITY OF THINKING

SOUL - CARD THREE REPRESENTS QUALITY OF ENERGY, YOUR INTERNAL DIRECTION AND GUIDANCE FOR THE DAY

PURPORT- as appears or is stated to be true but not necessarily true.

DAILY 3 CARD SPREAD

BODY – CARD ONE REPRESENTS YOUR EXTERNAL REALITY

MIND –CARD TWO REPRESENTS YOUR ATTITUDE, BELIEFS, AND QUALITY OF THINKING

SOUL – CARD THREE REPRESENTS QUALITY OF ENERGY, YOUR INTERNAL DIRECTION AND GUIDANCE FOR THE DAY

PURPORT– as appears or is stated to be true but not necessarily true.

DAILY 3 CARD SPREAD

BODY - CARD ONE REPRESENTS YOUR EXTERNAL REALITY

MIND -CARD TWO REPRESENTS YOUR ATTITUDE, BELIEFS, AND QUALITY OF THINKING

SOUL - CARD THREE REPRESENTS QUALITY OF ENERGY, YOUR INTERNAL DIRECTION AND GUIDANCE FOR THE DAY

PURPORT- as appears or is stated to be true but not necessarily true.

DAILY 3 CARD SPREAD

BODY - CARD ONE REPRESENTS YOUR EXTERNAL REALITY

MIND -CARD TWO REPRESENTS YOUR ATTITUDE, BELIEFS, AND QUALITY OF THINKING

SOUL - CARD THREE REPRESENTS QUALITY OF ENERGY, YOUR INTERNAL DIRECTION AND GUIDANCE FOR THE DAY

PURPORT- as appears or is stated to be true but not necessarily true.

DAILY 3 CARD SPREAD

BODY – CARD ONE REPRESENTS YOUR EXTERNAL REALITY

MIND –CARD TWO REPRESENTS YOUR ATTITUDE, BELIEFS, AND QUALITY OF THINKING

SOUL – CARD THREE REPRESENTS QUALITY OF ENERGY, YOUR INTERNAL DIRECTION AND GUIDANCE FOR THE DAY

PURPORT– as appears or is stated to be true but not necessarily true.

DAILY 3 CARD SPREAD

BODY – CARD ONE REPRESENTS YOUR EXTERNAL REALITY

MIND –CARD TWO REPRESENTS YOUR ATTITUDE, BELIEFS, AND QUALITY OF THINKING

SOUL – CARD THREE REPRESENTS QUALITY OF ENERGY, YOUR INTERNAL DIRECTION AND GUIDANCE FOR THE DAY

PURPORT– as appears or is stated to be true but not necessarily true.

DAILY 3 CARD SPREAD

BODY – CARD ONE REPRESENTS YOUR EXTERNAL REALITY

MIND –CARD TWO REPRESENTS YOUR ATTITUDE, BELIEFS, AND QUALITY OF THINKING

SOUL – CARD THREE REPRESENTS QUALITY OF ENERGY, YOUR INTERNAL DIRECTION AND GUIDANCE FOR THE DAY

PURPORT– as appears or is stated to be true but not necessarily true.

DAILY 3 CARD SPREAD

BODY – CARD ONE REPRESENTS YOUR EXTERNAL REALITY

MIND –CARD TWO REPRESENTS YOUR ATTITUDE, BELIEFS, AND QUALITY OF THINKING

SOUL – CARD THREE REPRESENTS QUALITY OF ENERGY, YOUR INTERNAL DIRECTION AND GUIDANCE FOR THE DAY

PURPORT– as appears or is stated to be true but not necessarily true.

DAILY 3 CARD SPREAD

BODY - CARD ONE REPRESENTS YOUR EXTERNAL REALITY

MIND -CARD TWO REPRESENTS YOUR ATTITUDE, BELIEFS, AND QUALITY OF THINKING

SOUL - CARD THREE REPRESENTS QUALITY OF ENERGY, YOUR INTERNAL DIRECTION AND GUIDANCE FOR THE DAY

PURPORT- as appears or is stated to be true but not necessarily true.

DAILY 3 CARD SPREAD

BODY - CARD ONE REPRESENTS YOUR EXTERNAL REALITY

MIND -CARD TWO REPRESENTS YOUR ATTITUDE, BELIEFS, AND QUALITY OF THINKING

SOUL - CARD THREE REPRESENTS QUALITY OF ENERGY, YOUR INTERNAL DIRECTION AND GUIDANCE FOR THE DAY

PURPORT- as appears or is stated to be true but not necessarily true.

DAILY 3 CARD SPREAD

BODY – CARD ONE REPRESENTS YOUR EXTERNAL REALITY

MIND –CARD TWO REPRESENTS YOUR ATTITUDE, BELIEFS, AND QUALITY OF THINKING

SOUL – CARD THREE REPRESENTS QUALITY OF ENERGY, YOUR INTERNAL DIRECTION AND GUIDANCE FOR THE DAY

PURPORT– as appears or is stated to be true but not necessarily true.

DAILY 3 CARD SPREAD

BODY - CARD ONE REPRESENTS YOUR EXTERNAL REALITY

MIND -CARD TWO REPRESENTS YOUR ATTITUDE, BELIEFS, AND QUALITY OF THINKING

SOUL - CARD THREE REPRESENTS QUALITY OF ENERGY, YOUR INTERNAL DIRECTION AND GUIDANCE FOR THE DAY

PURPORT- as appears or is stated to be true but not necessarily true.

DAILY 3 CARD SPREAD

BODY – CARD ONE REPRESENTS YOUR EXTERNAL REALITY

MIND –CARD TWO REPRESENTS YOUR ATTITUDE, BELIEFS, AND QUALITY OF THINKING

SOUL – CARD THREE REPRESENTS QUALITY OF ENERGY, YOUR INTERNAL DIRECTION AND GUIDANCE FOR THE DAY

PURPORT- as appears or is stated to be true but not necessarily true.

DAILY 3 CARD SPREAD

BODY - CARD ONE REPRESENTS YOUR EXTERNAL REALITY

MIND -CARD TWO REPRESENTS YOUR ATTITUDE, BELIEFS, AND QUALITY OF THINKING

SOUL - CARD THREE REPRESENTS QUALITY OF ENERGY, YOUR INTERNAL DIRECTION AND GUIDANCE FOR THE DAY

PURPORT- as appears or is stated to be true but not necessarily true.

DAILY 3 CARD SPREAD

BODY – CARD ONE REPRESENTS YOUR EXTERNAL REALITY

MIND – CARD TWO REPRESENTS YOUR ATTITUDE, BELIEFS, AND QUALITY OF THINKING

SOUL – CARD THREE REPRESENTS QUALITY OF ENERGY, YOUR INTERNAL DIRECTION AND GUIDANCE FOR THE DAY

PURPORT – as appears or is stated to be true but not necessarily true.

DAILY 3 CARD SPREAD

BODY – CARD ONE REPRESENTS YOUR EXTERNAL REALITY

MIND –CARD TWO REPRESENTS YOUR ATTITUDE, BELIEFS, AND QUALITY OF THINKING

SOUL – CARD THREE REPRESENTS QUALITY OF ENERGY, YOUR INTERNAL DIRECTION AND GUIDANCE FOR THE DAY

PURPORT– as appears or is stated to be true but not necessarily true.

DAILY 3 CARD SPREAD

BODY - CARD ONE REPRESENTS YOUR EXTERNAL REALITY

MIND -CARD TWO REPRESENTS YOUR ATTITUDE, BELIEFS, AND QUALITY OF THINKING

SOUL - CARD THREE REPRESENTS QUALITY OF ENERGY, YOUR INTERNAL DIRECTION AND GUIDANCE FOR THE DAY

PURPORT- as appears or is stated to be true but not necessarily true.

DAILY 3 CARD SPREAD

BODY - CARD ONE REPRESENTS YOUR EXTERNAL REALITY

MIND -CARD TWO REPRESENTS YOUR ATTITUDE, BELIEFS, AND QUALITY OF THINKING

SOUL - CARD THREE REPRESENTS QUALITY OF ENERGY, YOUR INTERNAL DIRECTION AND GUIDANCE FOR THE DAY

PURPORT- as appears or is stated to be true but not necessarily true.

DAILY 3 CARD SPREAD

BODY – CARD ONE REPRESENTS YOUR EXTERNAL REALITY

MIND –CARD TWO REPRESENTS YOUR ATTITUDE, BELIEFS, AND QUALITY OF THINKING

SOUL – CARD THREE REPRESENTS QUALITY OF ENERGY, YOUR INTERNAL DIRECTION AND GUIDANCE FOR THE DAY

PURPORT- as appears or is stated to be true but not necessarily true.

DAILY 3 CARD SPREAD

BODY – CARD ONE REPRESENTS YOUR EXTERNAL REALITY

MIND –CARD TWO REPRESENTS YOUR ATTITUDE, BELIEFS, AND QUALITY OF THINKING

SOUL – CARD THREE REPRESENTS QUALITY OF ENERGY, YOUR INTERNAL DIRECTION AND GUIDANCE FOR THE DAY

PURPORT– as appears or is stated to be true but not necessarily true.

DAILY 3 CARD SPREAD

BODY - CARD ONE REPRESENTS YOUR EXTERNAL REALITY

MIND -CARD TWO REPRESENTS YOUR ATTITUDE, BELIEFS, AND QUALITY OF THINKING

SOUL - CARD THREE REPRESENTS QUALITY OF ENERGY, YOUR INTERNAL DIRECTION AND GUIDANCE FOR THE DAY

PURPORT- as appears or is stated to be true but not necessarily true.

DAILY 3 CARD SPREAD

BODY - CARD ONE REPRESENTS YOUR EXTERNAL REALITY

MIND -CARD TWO REPRESENTS YOUR ATTITUDE, BELIEFS, AND QUALITY OF THINKING

SOUL - CARD THREE REPRESENTS QUALITY OF ENERGY, YOUR INTERNAL DIRECTION AND GUIDANCE FOR THE DAY

PURPORT- as appears or is stated to be true but not necessarily true.

DAILY 3 CARD SPREAD

BODY - CARD ONE REPRESENTS YOUR EXTERNAL REALITY

MIND -CARD TWO REPRESENTS YOUR ATTITUDE, BELIEFS, AND QUALITY OF THINKING

SOUL - CARD THREE REPRESENTS QUALITY OF ENERGY, YOUR INTERNAL DIRECTION AND GUIDANCE FOR THE DAY

PURPORT- as appears or is stated to be true but not necessarily true.

DAILY 3 CARD SPREAD

BODY - CARD ONE REPRESENTS YOUR EXTERNAL REALITY

MIND -CARD TWO REPRESENTS YOUR ATTITUDE, BELIEFS, AND QUALITY OF THINKING

SOUL - CARD THREE REPRESENTS QUALITY OF ENERGY, YOUR INTERNAL DIRECTION AND GUIDANCE FOR THE DAY

PURPORT- as appears or is stated to be true but not necessarily true.

DAILY 3 CARD SPREAD

BODY - CARD ONE REPRESENTS YOUR EXTERNAL REALITY

MIND -CARD TWO REPRESENTS YOUR ATTITUDE, BELIEFS, AND QUALITY OF THINKING

SOUL - CARD THREE REPRESENTS QUALITY OF ENERGY, YOUR INTERNAL DIRECTION AND GUIDANCE FOR THE DAY

PURPORT- as appears or is stated to be true but not necessarily true.

DAILY 3 CARD SPREAD

BODY – CARD ONE REPRESENTS YOUR EXTERNAL REALITY

MIND –CARD TWO REPRESENTS YOUR ATTITUDE, BELIEFS, AND QUALITY OF THINKING

SOUL – CARD THREE REPRESENTS QUALITY OF ENERGY, YOUR INTERNAL DIRECTION AND GUIDANCE FOR THE DAY

PURPORT– as appears or is stated to be true but not necessarily true.

DAILY 3 CARD SPREAD

BODY – CARD ONE REPRESENTS YOUR EXTERNAL REALITY

MIND –CARD TWO REPRESENTS YOUR ATTITUDE, BELIEFS, AND QUALITY OF THINKING

SOUL – CARD THREE REPRESENTS QUALITY OF ENERGY, YOUR INTERNAL DIRECTION AND GUIDANCE FOR THE DAY

PURPORT– as appears or is stated to be true but not necessarily true.

DAILY 3 CARD SPREAD

BODY - CARD ONE REPRESENTS YOUR EXTERNAL REALITY

MIND - CARD TWO REPRESENTS YOUR ATTITUDE, BELIEFS, AND QUALITY OF THINKING

SOUL - CARD THREE REPRESENTS QUALITY OF ENERGY, YOUR INTERNAL DIRECTION AND GUIDANCE FOR THE DAY

PURPORT- as appears or is stated to be true but not necessarily true.

DAILY 3 CARD SPREAD

BODY - CARD ONE REPRESENTS YOUR EXTERNAL REALITY

MIND -CARD TWO REPRESENTS YOUR ATTITUDE, BELIEFS, AND QUALITY OF THINKING

SOUL - CARD THREE REPRESENTS QUALITY OF ENERGY, YOUR INTERNAL DIRECTION AND GUIDANCE FOR THE DAY

PURPORT- as appears or is stated to be true but not necessarily true.

DAILY 3 CARD SPREAD

BODY - CARD ONE REPRESENTS YOUR EXTERNAL REALITY

MIND -CARD TWO REPRESENTS YOUR ATTITUDE, BELIEFS, AND QUALITY OF THINKING

SOUL - CARD THREE REPRESENTS QUALITY OF ENERGY, YOUR INTERNAL DIRECTION AND GUIDANCE FOR THE DAY

PURPORT- as appears or is stated to be true but not necessarily true.

DAILY 3 CARD SPREAD

BODY - CARD ONE REPRESENTS YOUR EXTERNAL REALITY

MIND -CARD TWO REPRESENTS YOUR ATTITUDE, BELIEFS, AND QUALITY OF THINKING

SOUL - CARD THREE REPRESENTS QUALITY OF ENERGY, YOUR INTERNAL DIRECTION AND GUIDANCE FOR THE DAY

PURPORT- as appears or is stated to be true but not necessarily true.

DAILY 3 CARD SPREAD

BODY – CARD ONE REPRESENTS YOUR EXTERNAL REALITY

MIND –CARD TWO REPRESENTS YOUR ATTITUDE, BELIEFS, AND QUALITY OF THINKING

SOUL – CARD THREE REPRESENTS QUALITY OF ENERGY, YOUR INTERNAL DIRECTION AND GUIDANCE FOR THE DAY

PURPORT– as appears or is stated to be true but not necessarily true.

DAILY 3 CARD SPREAD

BODY – CARD ONE REPRESENTS YOUR EXTERNAL REALITY

MIND –CARD TWO REPRESENTS YOUR ATTITUDE, BELIEFS, AND QUALITY OF THINKING

SOUL – CARD THREE REPRESENTS QUALITY OF ENERGY, YOUR INTERNAL DIRECTION AND GUIDANCE FOR THE DAY

PURPORT– as appears or is stated to be true but not necessarily true.

DAILY 3 CARD SPREAD

BODY - CARD ONE REPRESENTS YOUR EXTERNAL REALITY

MIND -CARD TWO REPRESENTS YOUR ATTITUDE, BELIEFS, AND QUALITY OF THINKING

SOUL - CARD THREE REPRESENTS QUALITY OF ENERGY, YOUR INTERNAL DIRECTION AND GUIDANCE FOR THE DAY

PURPORT- as appears or is stated to be true but not necessarily true.

DAILY 3 CARD SPREAD

BODY - CARD ONE REPRESENTS YOUR EXTERNAL REALITY

MIND -CARD TWO REPRESENTS YOUR ATTITUDE, BELIEFS, AND QUALITY OF THINKING

SOUL - CARD THREE REPRESENTS QUALITY OF ENERGY, YOUR INTERNAL DIRECTION AND GUIDANCE FOR THE DAY

PURPORT- as appears or is stated to be true but not necessarily true.

DAILY 3 CARD SPREAD

BODY – CARD ONE REPRESENTS YOUR EXTERNAL REALITY

MIND –CARD TWO REPRESENTS YOUR ATTITUDE, BELIEFS, AND QUALITY OF THINKING

SOUL – CARD THREE REPRESENTS QUALITY OF ENERGY, YOUR INTERNAL DIRECTION AND GUIDANCE FOR THE DAY

PURPORT– as appears or is stated to be true but not necessarily true.

DAILY 3 CARD SPREAD

BODY – CARD ONE REPRESENTS YOUR EXTERNAL REALITY

MIND –CARD TWO REPRESENTS YOUR ATTITUDE, BELIEFS, AND QUALITY OF THINKING

SOUL – CARD THREE REPRESENTS QUALITY OF ENERGY, YOUR INTERNAL DIRECTION AND GUIDANCE FOR THE DAY

PURPORT– as appears or is stated to be true but not necessarily true.

DAILY 3 CARD SPREAD

BODY - CARD ONE REPRESENTS YOUR EXTERNAL REALITY

MIND -CARD TWO REPRESENTS YOUR ATTITUDE, BELIEFS, AND QUALITY OF THINKING

SOUL - CARD THREE REPRESENTS QUALITY OF ENERGY, YOUR INTERNAL DIRECTION AND GUIDANCE FOR THE DAY

PURPORT- as appears or is stated to be true but not necessarily true.

DAILY 3 CARD SPREAD

BODY - CARD ONE REPRESENTS YOUR EXTERNAL REALITY

MIND -CARD TWO REPRESENTS YOUR ATTITUDE, BELIEFS, AND QUALITY OF THINKING

SOUL - CARD THREE REPRESENTS QUALITY OF ENERGY, YOUR INTERNAL DIRECTION AND GUIDANCE FOR THE DAY

PURPORT- as appears or is stated to be true but not necessarily true.

DAILY 3 CARD SPREAD

BODY – CARD ONE REPRESENTS YOUR EXTERNAL REALITY

MIND –CARD TWO REPRESENTS YOUR ATTITUDE, BELIEFS, AND QUALITY OF THINKING

SOUL – CARD THREE REPRESENTS QUALITY OF ENERGY, YOUR INTERNAL DIRECTION AND GUIDANCE FOR THE DAY

PURPORT– as appears or is stated to be true but not necessarily true.

DAILY 3 CARD SPREAD

BODY - CARD ONE REPRESENTS YOUR EXTERNAL REALITY

MIND -CARD TWO REPRESENTS YOUR ATTITUDE, BELIEFS, AND QUALITY OF THINKING

SOUL - CARD THREE REPRESENTS QUALITY OF ENERGY, YOUR INTERNAL DIRECTION AND GUIDANCE FOR THE DAY

PURPORT- as appears or is stated to be true but not necessarily true.

DAILY 3 CARD SPREAD

BODY - CARD ONE REPRESENTS YOUR EXTERNAL REALITY

MIND -CARD TWO REPRESENTS YOUR ATTITUDE, BELIEFS, AND QUALITY OF THINKING

SOUL - CARD THREE REPRESENTS QUALITY OF ENERGY, YOUR INTERNAL DIRECTION AND GUIDANCE FOR THE DAY

PURPORT- as appears or is stated to be true but not necessarily true.

DAILY 3 CARD SPREAD

BODY – CARD ONE REPRESENTS YOUR EXTERNAL REALITY

MIND –CARD TWO REPRESENTS YOUR ATTITUDE, BELIEFS, AND QUALITY OF THINKING

SOUL – CARD THREE REPRESENTS QUALITY OF ENERGY, YOUR INTERNAL DIRECTION AND GUIDANCE FOR THE DAY

PURPORT– as appears or is stated to be true but not necessarily true.

DAILY 3 CARD SPREAD

BODY - CARD ONE REPRESENTS YOUR EXTERNAL REALITY

MIND -CARD TWO REPRESENTS YOUR ATTITUDE, BELIEFS, AND QUALITY OF THINKING

SOUL - CARD THREE REPRESENTS QUALITY OF ENERGY, YOUR INTERNAL DIRECTION AND GUIDANCE FOR THE DAY

PURPORT- as appears or is stated to be true but not necessarily true.

DAILY 3 CARD SPREAD

BODY – CARD ONE REPRESENTS YOUR EXTERNAL REALITY

MIND –CARD TWO REPRESENTS YOUR ATTITUDE, BELIEFS, AND QUALITY OF THINKING

SOUL – CARD THREE REPRESENTS QUALITY OF ENERGY, YOUR INTERNAL DIRECTION AND GUIDANCE FOR THE DAY

PURPORT– as appears or is stated to be true but not necessarily true.

DAILY 3 CARD SPREAD

BODY - CARD ONE REPRESENTS YOUR EXTERNAL REALITY

MIND -CARD TWO REPRESENTS YOUR ATTITUDE, BELIEFS, AND QUALITY OF THINKING

SOUL - CARD THREE REPRESENTS QUALITY OF ENERGY, YOUR INTERNAL DIRECTION AND GUIDANCE FOR THE DAY

PURPORT- as appears or is stated to be true but not necessarily true.

DAILY 3 CARD SPREAD

BODY – CARD ONE REPRESENTS YOUR EXTERNAL REALITY

MIND –CARD TWO REPRESENTS YOUR ATTITUDE, BELIEFS, AND QUALITY OF THINKING

SOUL – CARD THREE REPRESENTS QUALITY OF ENERGY, YOUR INTERNAL DIRECTION AND GUIDANCE FOR THE DAY

PURPORT– as appears or is stated to be true but not necessarily true.

DAILY 3 CARD SPREAD

BODY - CARD ONE REPRESENTS YOUR EXTERNAL REALITY

MIND -CARD TWO REPRESENTS YOUR ATTITUDE, BELIEFS, AND QUALITY OF THINKING

SOUL - CARD THREE REPRESENTS QUALITY OF ENERGY, YOUR INTERNAL DIRECTION AND GUIDANCE FOR THE DAY

PURPORT- as appears or is stated to be true but not necessarily true.

DAILY 3 CARD SPREAD

BODY - CARD ONE REPRESENTS YOUR EXTERNAL REALITY

MIND -CARD TWO REPRESENTS YOUR ATTITUDE, BELIEFS, AND QUALITY OF THINKING

SOUL - CARD THREE REPRESENTS QUALITY OF ENERGY, YOUR INTERNAL DIRECTION AND GUIDANCE FOR THE DAY

PURPORT- as appears or is stated to be true but not necessarily true.

DAILY 3 CARD SPREAD

BODY – CARD ONE REPRESENTS YOUR EXTERNAL REALITY

MIND –CARD TWO REPRESENTS YOUR ATTITUDE, BELIEFS, AND QUALITY OF THINKING

SOUL – CARD THREE REPRESENTS QUALITY OF ENERGY, YOUR INTERNAL DIRECTION AND GUIDANCE FOR THE DAY

PURPORT– as appears or is stated to be true but not necessarily true.

DAILY 3 CARD SPREAD

BODY – CARD ONE REPRESENTS YOUR EXTERNAL REALITY

MIND –CARD TWO REPRESENTS YOUR ATTITUDE, BELIEFS, AND QUALITY OF THINKING

SOUL – CARD THREE REPRESENTS QUALITY OF ENERGY, YOUR INTERNAL DIRECTION AND GUIDANCE FOR THE DAY

PURPORT– as appears or is stated to be true but not necessarily true.

DAILY 3 CARD SPREAD

BODY - CARD ONE REPRESENTS YOUR EXTERNAL REALITY

MIND -CARD TWO REPRESENTS YOUR ATTITUDE, BELIEFS, AND QUALITY OF THINKING

SOUL - CARD THREE REPRESENTS QUALITY OF ENERGY, YOUR INTERNAL DIRECTION AND GUIDANCE FOR THE DAY

PURPORT- as appears or is stated to be true but not necessarily true.

DAILY 3 CARD SPREAD

BODY – CARD ONE REPRESENTS YOUR EXTERNAL REALITY

MIND –CARD TWO REPRESENTS YOUR ATTITUDE, BELIEFS, AND QUALITY OF THINKING

SOUL – CARD THREE REPRESENTS QUALITY OF ENERGY, YOUR INTERNAL DIRECTION AND GUIDANCE FOR THE DAY

PURPORT– as appears or is stated to be true but not necessarily true.

DAILY 3 CARD SPREAD

BODY - CARD ONE REPRESENTS YOUR EXTERNAL REALITY

MIND -CARD TWO REPRESENTS YOUR ATTITUDE, BELIEFS, AND QUALITY OF THINKING

SOUL - CARD THREE REPRESENTS QUALITY OF ENERGY, YOUR INTERNAL DIRECTION AND GUIDANCE FOR THE DAY

PURPORT- as appears or is stated to be true but not necessarily true.

DAILY 3 CARD SPREAD

BODY – CARD ONE REPRESENTS YOUR EXTERNAL REALITY

MIND –CARD TWO REPRESENTS YOUR ATTITUDE, BELIEFS, AND QUALITY OF THINKING

SOUL – CARD THREE REPRESENTS QUALITY OF ENERGY, YOUR INTERNAL DIRECTION AND GUIDANCE FOR THE DAY

PURPORT- as appears or is stated to be true but not necessarily true.

DAILY 3 CARD SPREAD

BODY - CARD ONE REPRESENTS YOUR EXTERNAL REALITY

MIND -CARD TWO REPRESENTS YOUR ATTITUDE, BELIEFS, AND QUALITY OF THINKING

SOUL - CARD THREE REPRESENTS QUALITY OF ENERGY, YOUR INTERNAL DIRECTION AND GUIDANCE FOR THE DAY

PURPORT- as appears or is stated to be true but not necessarily true.

DAILY 3 CARD SPREAD

BODY – CARD ONE REPRESENTS YOUR EXTERNAL REALITY

MIND – CARD TWO REPRESENTS YOUR ATTITUDE, BELIEFS, AND QUALITY OF THINKING

SOUL – CARD THREE REPRESENTS QUALITY OF ENERGY, YOUR INTERNAL DIRECTION AND GUIDANCE FOR THE DAY

PURPORT– as appears or is stated to be true but not necessarily true.

DAILY 3 CARD SPREAD

BODY – CARD ONE REPRESENTS YOUR EXTERNAL REALITY

MIND –CARD TWO REPRESENTS YOUR ATTITUDE, BELIEFS, AND QUALITY OF THINKING

SOUL – CARD THREE REPRESENTS QUALITY OF ENERGY, YOUR INTERNAL DIRECTION AND GUIDANCE FOR THE DAY

PURPORT- as appears or is stated to be true but not necessarily true.

DAILY 3 CARD SPREAD

BODY - CARD ONE REPRESENTS YOUR EXTERNAL REALITY

MIND -CARD TWO REPRESENTS YOUR ATTITUDE, BELIEFS, AND QUALITY OF THINKING

SOUL - CARD THREE REPRESENTS QUALITY OF ENERGY, YOUR INTERNAL DIRECTION AND GUIDANCE FOR THE DAY

PURPORT- as appears or is stated to be true but not necessarily true.

DAILY 3 CARD SPREAD

BODY - CARD ONE REPRESENTS YOUR EXTERNAL REALITY

MIND -CARD TWO REPRESENTS YOUR ATTITUDE, BELIEFS, AND QUALITY OF THINKING

SOUL - CARD THREE REPRESENTS QUALITY OF ENERGY, YOUR INTERNAL DIRECTION AND GUIDANCE FOR THE DAY

PURPORT- as appears or is stated to be true but not necessarily true.

DAILY 3 CARD SPREAD

BODY - CARD ONE REPRESENTS YOUR EXTERNAL REALITY

MIND -CARD TWO REPRESENTS YOUR ATTITUDE, BELIEFS, AND QUALITY OF THINKING

SOUL - CARD THREE REPRESENTS QUALITY OF ENERGY, YOUR INTERNAL DIRECTION AND GUIDANCE FOR THE DAY

PURPORT- as appears or is stated to be true but not necessarily true.

DAILY 3 CARD SPREAD

BODY - CARD ONE REPRESENTS YOUR EXTERNAL REALITY

MIND - CARD TWO REPRESENTS YOUR ATTITUDE, BELIEFS, AND QUALITY OF THINKING

SOUL - CARD THREE REPRESENTS QUALITY OF ENERGY, YOUR INTERNAL DIRECTION AND GUIDANCE FOR THE DAY

PURPORT- as appears or is stated to be true but not necessarily true.

DAILY 3 CARD SPREAD

BODY - CARD ONE REPRESENTS YOUR EXTERNAL REALITY

MIND -CARD TWO REPRESENTS YOUR ATTITUDE, BELIEFS, AND QUALITY OF THINKING

SOUL - CARD THREE REPRESENTS QUALITY OF ENERGY, YOUR INTERNAL DIRECTION AND GUIDANCE FOR THE DAY

PURPORT- as appears or is stated to be true but not necessarily true.

DAILY 3 CARD SPREAD

BODY - CARD ONE REPRESENTS YOUR EXTERNAL REALITY

MIND -CARD TWO REPRESENTS YOUR ATTITUDE, BELIEFS, AND QUALITY OF THINKING

SOUL - CARD THREE REPRESENTS QUALITY OF ENERGY, YOUR INTERNAL DIRECTION AND GUIDANCE FOR THE DAY

PURPORT- as appears or is stated to be true but not necessarily true.

DAILY 3 CARD SPREAD

BODY - CARD ONE REPRESENTS YOUR EXTERNAL REALITY

MIND -CARD TWO REPRESENTS YOUR ATTITUDE, BELIEFS, AND QUALITY OF THINKING

SOUL - CARD THREE REPRESENTS QUALITY OF ENERGY, YOUR INTERNAL DIRECTION AND GUIDANCE FOR THE DAY

PURPORT- as appears or is stated to be true but not necessarily true.

DAILY 3 CARD SPREAD

BODY - CARD ONE REPRESENTS YOUR EXTERNAL REALITY

MIND -CARD TWO REPRESENTS YOUR ATTITUDE, BELIEFS, AND QUALITY OF THINKING

SOUL - CARD THREE REPRESENTS QUALITY OF ENERGY, YOUR INTERNAL DIRECTION AND GUIDANCE FOR THE DAY

PURPORT- as appears or is stated to be true but not necessarily true.

DAILY 3 CARD SPREAD

BODY - CARD ONE REPRESENTS YOUR EXTERNAL REALITY

MIND -CARD TWO REPRESENTS YOUR ATTITUDE, BELIEFS, AND QUALITY OF THINKING

SOUL - CARD THREE REPRESENTS QUALITY OF ENERGY, YOUR INTERNAL DIRECTION AND GUIDANCE FOR THE DAY

PURPORT- as appears or is stated to be true but not necessarily true.

DAILY 3 CARD SPREAD

BODY - CARD ONE REPRESENTS YOUR EXTERNAL REALITY

MIND -CARD TWO REPRESENTS YOUR ATTITUDE, BELIEFS, AND QUALITY OF THINKING

SOUL - CARD THREE REPRESENTS QUALITY OF ENERGY, YOUR INTERNAL DIRECTION AND GUIDANCE FOR THE DAY

PURPORT- as appears or is stated to be true but not necessarily true.

DAILY 3 CARD SPREAD

BODY - CARD ONE REPRESENTS YOUR EXTERNAL REALITY

MIND -CARD TWO REPRESENTS YOUR ATTITUDE, BELIEFS, AND QUALITY OF THINKING

SOUL - CARD THREE REPRESENTS QUALITY OF ENERGY, YOUR INTERNAL DIRECTION AND GUIDANCE FOR THE DAY

PURPORT- as appears or is stated to be true but not necessarily true.

DAILY 3 CARD SPREAD

BODY – CARD ONE REPRESENTS YOUR EXTERNAL REALITY

MIND –CARD TWO REPRESENTS YOUR ATTITUDE, BELIEFS, AND QUALITY OF THINKING

SOUL – CARD THREE REPRESENTS QUALITY OF ENERGY, YOUR INTERNAL DIRECTION AND GUIDANCE FOR THE DAY

PURPORT– as appears or is stated to be true but not necessarily true.

DAILY 3 CARD SPREAD

BODY – CARD ONE REPRESENTS YOUR EXTERNAL REALITY

MIND –CARD TWO REPRESENTS YOUR ATTITUDE, BELIEFS, AND QUALITY OF THINKING

SOUL – CARD THREE REPRESENTS QUALITY OF ENERGY, YOUR INTERNAL DIRECTION AND GUIDANCE FOR THE DAY

PURPORT– as appears or is stated to be true but not necessarily true.

DAILY 3 CARD SPREAD

BODY - CARD ONE REPRESENTS YOUR EXTERNAL REALITY

MIND -CARD TWO REPRESENTS YOUR ATTITUDE, BELIEFS, AND QUALITY OF THINKING

SOUL - CARD THREE REPRESENTS QUALITY OF ENERGY, YOUR INTERNAL DIRECTION AND GUIDANCE FOR THE DAY

PURPORT- as appears or is stated to be true but not necessarily true.

DAILY 3 CARD SPREAD

BODY – CARD ONE REPRESENTS YOUR EXTERNAL REALITY

MIND –CARD TWO REPRESENTS YOUR ATTITUDE, BELIEFS, AND QUALITY OF THINKING

SOUL – CARD THREE REPRESENTS QUALITY OF ENERGY, YOUR INTERNAL DIRECTION AND GUIDANCE FOR THE DAY

PURPORT– as appears or is stated to be true but not necessarily true.

DAILY 3 CARD SPREAD

BODY - CARD ONE REPRESENTS YOUR EXTERNAL REALITY

MIND -CARD TWO REPRESENTS YOUR ATTITUDE, BELIEFS, AND QUALITY OF THINKING

SOUL - CARD THREE REPRESENTS QUALITY OF ENERGY, YOUR INTERNAL DIRECTION AND GUIDANCE FOR THE DAY

PURPORT- as appears or is stated to be true but not necessarily true.

DAILY 3 CARD SPREAD

BODY - CARD ONE REPRESENTS YOUR EXTERNAL REALITY

MIND -CARD TWO REPRESENTS YOUR ATTITUDE, BELIEFS, AND QUALITY OF THINKING

SOUL - CARD THREE REPRESENTS QUALITY OF ENERGY, YOUR INTERNAL DIRECTION AND GUIDANCE FOR THE DAY

PURPORT- as appears or is stated to be true but not necessarily true.

DAILY 3 CARD SPREAD

BODY - CARD ONE REPRESENTS YOUR EXTERNAL REALITY

MIND -CARD TWO REPRESENTS YOUR ATTITUDE, BELIEFS, AND QUALITY OF THINKING

SOUL - CARD THREE REPRESENTS QUALITY OF ENERGY, YOUR INTERNAL DIRECTION AND GUIDANCE FOR THE DAY

PURPORT- as appears or is stated to be true but not necessarily true.

DAILY 3 CARD SPREAD

BODY – CARD ONE REPRESENTS YOUR EXTERNAL REALITY

MIND –CARD TWO REPRESENTS YOUR ATTITUDE, BELIEFS, AND QUALITY OF THINKING

SOUL – CARD THREE REPRESENTS QUALITY OF ENERGY, YOUR INTERNAL DIRECTION AND GUIDANCE FOR THE DAY

PURPORT– as appears or is stated to be true but not necessarily true.

DAILY 3 CARD SPREAD

BODY - CARD ONE REPRESENTS YOUR EXTERNAL REALITY

MIND -CARD TWO REPRESENTS YOUR ATTITUDE, BELIEFS, AND QUALITY OF THINKING

SOUL - CARD THREE REPRESENTS QUALITY OF ENERGY, YOUR INTERNAL DIRECTION AND GUIDANCE FOR THE DAY

PURPORT- as appears or is stated to be true but not necessarily true.

DAILY 3 CARD SPREAD

BODY – CARD ONE REPRESENTS YOUR EXTERNAL REALITY

MIND –CARD TWO REPRESENTS YOUR ATTITUDE, BELIEFS, AND QUALITY OF THINKING

SOUL – CARD THREE REPRESENTS QUALITY OF ENERGY, YOUR INTERNAL DIRECTION AND GUIDANCE FOR THE DAY

PURPORT– as appears or is stated to be true but not necessarily true.

DAILY 3 CARD SPREAD

BODY - CARD ONE REPRESENTS YOUR EXTERNAL REALITY

MIND -CARD TWO REPRESENTS YOUR ATTITUDE, BELIEFS, AND QUALITY OF THINKING

SOUL - CARD THREE REPRESENTS QUALITY OF ENERGY, YOUR INTERNAL DIRECTION AND GUIDANCE FOR THE DAY

PURPORT- as appears or is stated to be true but not necessarily true.

DAILY 3 CARD SPREAD

BODY – CARD ONE REPRESENTS YOUR EXTERNAL REALITY

MIND –CARD TWO REPRESENTS YOUR ATTITUDE, BELIEFS, AND QUALITY OF THINKING

SOUL – CARD THREE REPRESENTS QUALITY OF ENERGY, YOUR INTERNAL DIRECTION AND GUIDANCE FOR THE DAY

PURPORT– as appears or is stated to be true but not necessarily true.

DAILY 3 CARD SPREAD

BODY - CARD ONE REPRESENTS YOUR EXTERNAL REALITY

MIND -CARD TWO REPRESENTS YOUR ATTITUDE, BELIEFS, AND QUALITY OF THINKING

SOUL - CARD THREE REPRESENTS QUALITY OF ENERGY, YOUR INTERNAL DIRECTION AND GUIDANCE FOR THE DAY

PURPORT- as appears or is stated to be true but not necessarily true.

DAILY 3 CARD SPREAD

BODY - CARD ONE REPRESENTS YOUR EXTERNAL REALITY

MIND -CARD TWO REPRESENTS YOUR ATTITUDE, BELIEFS, AND QUALITY OF THINKING

SOUL - CARD THREE REPRESENTS QUALITY OF ENERGY, YOUR INTERNAL DIRECTION AND GUIDANCE FOR THE DAY

PURPORT- as appears or is stated to be true but not necessarily true.

DAILY 3 CARD SPREAD

BODY - CARD ONE REPRESENTS YOUR EXTERNAL REALITY

MIND -CARD TWO REPRESENTS YOUR ATTITUDE, BELIEFS, AND QUALITY OF THINKING

SOUL - CARD THREE REPRESENTS QUALITY OF ENERGY, YOUR INTERNAL DIRECTION AND GUIDANCE FOR THE DAY

PURPORT- as appears or is stated to be true but not necessarily true.

DAILY 3 CARD SPREAD

BODY - CARD ONE REPRESENTS YOUR EXTERNAL REALITY

MIND -CARD TWO REPRESENTS YOUR ATTITUDE, BELIEFS, AND QUALITY OF THINKING

SOUL - CARD THREE REPRESENTS QUALITY OF ENERGY, YOUR INTERNAL DIRECTION AND GUIDANCE FOR THE DAY

PURPORT- as appears or is stated to be true but not necessarily true.

DAILY 3 CARD SPREAD

BODY - CARD ONE REPRESENTS YOUR EXTERNAL REALITY

MIND -CARD TWO REPRESENTS YOUR ATTITUDE, BELIEFS, AND QUALITY OF THINKING

SOUL - CARD THREE REPRESENTS QUALITY OF ENERGY, YOUR INTERNAL DIRECTION AND GUIDANCE FOR THE DAY

PURPORT- as appears or is stated to be true but not necessarily true.

DAILY 3 CARD SPREAD

BODY - CARD ONE REPRESENTS YOUR EXTERNAL REALITY

MIND -CARD TWO REPRESENTS YOUR ATTITUDE, BELIEFS, AND QUALITY OF THINKING

SOUL - CARD THREE REPRESENTS QUALITY OF ENERGY, YOUR INTERNAL DIRECTION AND GUIDANCE FOR THE DAY

PURPORT- as appears or is stated to be true but not necessarily true.

DAILY 3 CARD SPREAD

BODY - CARD ONE REPRESENTS YOUR EXTERNAL REALITY

MIND -CARD TWO REPRESENTS YOUR ATTITUDE, BELIEFS, AND QUALITY OF THINKING

SOUL - CARD THREE REPRESENTS QUALITY OF ENERGY, YOUR INTERNAL DIRECTION AND GUIDANCE FOR THE DAY

PURPORT- as appears or is stated to be true but not necessarily true.

DAILY 3 CARD SPREAD

BODY – CARD ONE REPRESENTS YOUR EXTERNAL REALITY

MIND –CARD TWO REPRESENTS YOUR ATTITUDE, BELIEFS, AND QUALITY OF THINKING

SOUL – CARD THREE REPRESENTS QUALITY OF ENERGY, YOUR INTERNAL DIRECTION AND GUIDANCE FOR THE DAY

PURPORT– as appears or is stated to be true but not necessarily true.

DAILY 3 CARD SPREAD

BODY - CARD ONE REPRESENTS YOUR EXTERNAL REALITY

MIND -CARD TWO REPRESENTS YOUR ATTITUDE, BELIEFS, AND QUALITY OF THINKING

SOUL - CARD THREE REPRESENTS QUALITY OF ENERGY, YOUR INTERNAL DIRECTION AND GUIDANCE FOR THE DAY

PURPORT- as appears or is stated to be true but not necessarily true.

DAILY 3 CARD SPREAD

BODY - CARD ONE REPRESENTS YOUR EXTERNAL REALITY

MIND -CARD TWO REPRESENTS YOUR ATTITUDE, BELIEFS, AND QUALITY OF THINKING

SOUL - CARD THREE REPRESENTS QUALITY OF ENERGY, YOUR INTERNAL DIRECTION AND GUIDANCE FOR THE DAY

PURPORT- as appears or is stated to be true but not necessarily true.

DAILY 3 CARD SPREAD

BODY – CARD ONE REPRESENTS YOUR EXTERNAL REALITY

MIND –CARD TWO REPRESENTS YOUR ATTITUDE, BELIEFS, AND QUALITY OF THINKING

SOUL – CARD THREE REPRESENTS QUALITY OF ENERGY, YOUR INTERNAL DIRECTION AND GUIDANCE FOR THE DAY

PURPORT– as appears or is stated to be true but not necessarily true.

DAILY 3 CARD SPREAD

BODY – CARD ONE REPRESENTS YOUR EXTERNAL REALITY

MIND –CARD TWO REPRESENTS YOUR ATTITUDE, BELIEFS, AND QUALITY OF THINKING

SOUL – CARD THREE REPRESENTS QUALITY OF ENERGY, YOUR INTERNAL DIRECTION AND GUIDANCE FOR THE DAY

PURPORT– as appears or is stated to be true but not necessarily true.

DAILY 3 CARD SPREAD

BODY - CARD ONE REPRESENTS YOUR EXTERNAL REALITY

MIND -CARD TWO REPRESENTS YOUR ATTITUDE, BELIEFS, AND QUALITY OF THINKING

SOUL - CARD THREE REPRESENTS QUALITY OF ENERGY, YOUR INTERNAL DIRECTION AND GUIDANCE FOR THE DAY

PURPORT- as appears or is stated to be true but not necessarily true.

DAILY 3 CARD SPREAD

BODY - CARD ONE REPRESENTS YOUR EXTERNAL REALITY

MIND - CARD TWO REPRESENTS YOUR ATTITUDE, BELIEFS, AND QUALITY OF THINKING

SOUL - CARD THREE REPRESENTS QUALITY OF ENERGY, YOUR INTERNAL DIRECTION AND GUIDANCE FOR THE DAY

PURPORT- as appears or is stated to be true but not necessarily true.

DAILY 3 CARD SPREAD

BODY - CARD ONE REPRESENTS YOUR EXTERNAL REALITY

MIND -CARD TWO REPRESENTS YOUR ATTITUDE, BELIEFS, AND QUALITY OF THINKING

SOUL - CARD THREE REPRESENTS QUALITY OF ENERGY, YOUR INTERNAL DIRECTION AND GUIDANCE FOR THE DAY

PURPORT- as appears or is stated to be true but not necessarily true.

DAILY 3 CARD SPREAD

BODY – CARD ONE REPRESENTS YOUR EXTERNAL REALITY

MIND –CARD TWO REPRESENTS YOUR ATTITUDE, BELIEFS, AND QUALITY OF THINKING

SOUL – CARD THREE REPRESENTS QUALITY OF ENERGY, YOUR INTERNAL DIRECTION AND GUIDANCE FOR THE DAY

PURPORT– as appears or is stated to be true but not necessarily true.

DAILY 3 CARD SPREAD

BODY - CARD ONE REPRESENTS YOUR EXTERNAL REALITY

MIND -CARD TWO REPRESENTS YOUR ATTITUDE, BELIEFS, AND QUALITY OF THINKING

SOUL - CARD THREE REPRESENTS QUALITY OF ENERGY, YOUR INTERNAL DIRECTION AND GUIDANCE FOR THE DAY

PURPORT- as appears or is stated to be true but not necessarily true.

DAILY 3 CARD SPREAD

BODY - CARD ONE REPRESENTS YOUR EXTERNAL REALITY

MIND -CARD TWO REPRESENTS YOUR ATTITUDE, BELIEFS, AND QUALITY OF THINKING

SOUL - CARD THREE REPRESENTS QUALITY OF ENERGY, YOUR INTERNAL DIRECTION AND GUIDANCE FOR THE DAY

PURPORT- as appears or is stated to be true but not necessarily true.

DAILY 3 CARD SPREAD

BODY - CARD ONE REPRESENTS YOUR EXTERNAL REALITY

MIND -CARD TWO REPRESENTS YOUR ATTITUDE, BELIEFS, AND QUALITY OF THINKING

SOUL - CARD THREE REPRESENTS QUALITY OF ENERGY, YOUR INTERNAL DIRECTION AND GUIDANCE FOR THE DAY

PURPORT- as appears or is stated to be true but not necessarily true.

DAILY 3 CARD SPREAD

BODY - CARD ONE REPRESENTS YOUR EXTERNAL REALITY

MIND -CARD TWO REPRESENTS YOUR ATTITUDE, BELIEFS, AND QUALITY OF THINKING

SOUL - CARD THREE REPRESENTS QUALITY OF ENERGY, YOUR INTERNAL DIRECTION AND GUIDANCE FOR THE DAY

PURPORT- as appears or is stated to be true but not necessarily true.

DAILY 3 CARD SPREAD

BODY - CARD ONE REPRESENTS YOUR EXTERNAL REALITY

MIND -CARD TWO REPRESENTS YOUR ATTITUDE, BELIEFS, AND QUALITY OF THINKING

SOUL - CARD THREE REPRESENTS QUALITY OF ENERGY, YOUR INTERNAL DIRECTION AND GUIDANCE FOR THE DAY

PURPORT- as appears or is stated to be true but not necessarily true.

DAILY 3 CARD SPREAD

BODY - CARD ONE REPRESENTS YOUR EXTERNAL REALITY

MIND -CARD TWO REPRESENTS YOUR ATTITUDE, BELIEFS, AND QUALITY OF THINKING

SOUL - CARD THREE REPRESENTS QUALITY OF ENERGY, YOUR INTERNAL DIRECTION AND GUIDANCE FOR THE DAY

PURPORT- as appears or is stated to be true but not necessarily true.

DAILY 3 CARD SPREAD

BODY - CARD ONE REPRESENTS YOUR EXTERNAL REALITY

MIND -CARD TWO REPRESENTS YOUR ATTITUDE, BELIEFS, AND QUALITY OF THINKING

SOUL - CARD THREE REPRESENTS QUALITY OF ENERGY, YOUR INTERNAL DIRECTION AND GUIDANCE FOR THE DAY

PURPORT- as appears or is stated to be true but not necessarily true.

DAILY 3 CARD SPREAD

BODY – CARD ONE REPRESENTS YOUR EXTERNAL REALITY

MIND –CARD TWO REPRESENTS YOUR ATTITUDE, BELIEFS, AND QUALITY OF THINKING

SOUL – CARD THREE REPRESENTS QUALITY OF ENERGY, YOUR INTERNAL DIRECTION AND GUIDANCE FOR THE DAY

PURPORT– as appears or is stated to be true but not necessarily true.

DAILY 3 CARD SPREAD

BODY - CARD ONE REPRESENTS YOUR EXTERNAL REALITY

MIND -CARD TWO REPRESENTS YOUR ATTITUDE, BELIEFS, AND QUALITY OF THINKING

SOUL - CARD THREE REPRESENTS QUALITY OF ENERGY, YOUR INTERNAL DIRECTION AND GUIDANCE FOR THE DAY

PURPORT- as appears or is stated to be true but not necessarily true.

DAILY 3 CARD SPREAD

BODY - CARD ONE REPRESENTS YOUR EXTERNAL REALITY

MIND -CARD TWO REPRESENTS YOUR ATTITUDE, BELIEFS, AND QUALITY OF THINKING

SOUL - CARD THREE REPRESENTS QUALITY OF ENERGY, YOUR INTERNAL DIRECTION AND GUIDANCE FOR THE DAY

PURPORT- as appears or is stated to be true but not necessarily true.

DAILY 3 CARD SPREAD

BODY - CARD ONE REPRESENTS YOUR EXTERNAL REALITY

MIND -CARD TWO REPRESENTS YOUR ATTITUDE, BELIEFS, AND QUALITY OF THINKING

SOUL - CARD THREE REPRESENTS QUALITY OF ENERGY, YOUR INTERNAL DIRECTION AND GUIDANCE FOR THE DAY

PURPORT- as appears or is stated to be true but not necessarily true.

DAILY 3 CARD SPREAD

BODY - CARD ONE REPRESENTS YOUR EXTERNAL REALITY

MIND -CARD TWO REPRESENTS YOUR ATTITUDE, BELIEFS, AND QUALITY OF THINKING

SOUL - CARD THREE REPRESENTS QUALITY OF ENERGY, YOUR INTERNAL DIRECTION AND GUIDANCE FOR THE DAY

PURPORT- as appears or is stated to be true but not necessarily true.

DAILY 3 CARD SPREAD

BODY – CARD ONE REPRESENTS YOUR EXTERNAL REALITY

MIND –CARD TWO REPRESENTS YOUR ATTITUDE, BELIEFS, AND QUALITY OF THINKING

SOUL – CARD THREE REPRESENTS QUALITY OF ENERGY, YOUR INTERNAL DIRECTION AND GUIDANCE FOR THE DAY

PURPORT– as appears or is stated to be true but not necessarily true.

DAILY 3 CARD SPREAD

BODY – CARD ONE REPRESENTS YOUR EXTERNAL REALITY

MIND –CARD TWO REPRESENTS YOUR ATTITUDE, BELIEFS, AND QUALITY OF THINKING

SOUL – CARD THREE REPRESENTS QUALITY OF ENERGY, YOUR INTERNAL DIRECTION AND GUIDANCE FOR THE DAY

PURPORT– as appears or is stated to be true but not necessarily true.

DAILY 3 CARD SPREAD

BODY - CARD ONE REPRESENTS YOUR EXTERNAL REALITY

MIND -CARD TWO REPRESENTS YOUR ATTITUDE, BELIEFS, AND QUALITY OF THINKING

SOUL - CARD THREE REPRESENTS QUALITY OF ENERGY, YOUR INTERNAL DIRECTION AND GUIDANCE FOR THE DAY

PURPORT- as appears or is stated to be true but not necessarily true.

DAILY 3 CARD SPREAD

BODY - CARD ONE REPRESENTS YOUR EXTERNAL REALITY

MIND -CARD TWO REPRESENTS YOUR ATTITUDE, BELIEFS, AND QUALITY OF THINKING

SOUL - CARD THREE REPRESENTS QUALITY OF ENERGY, YOUR INTERNAL DIRECTION AND GUIDANCE FOR THE DAY

PURPORT- as appears or is stated to be true but not necessarily true.

DAILY 3 CARD SPREAD

BODY - CARD ONE REPRESENTS YOUR EXTERNAL REALITY

MIND -CARD TWO REPRESENTS YOUR ATTITUDE, BELIEFS, AND QUALITY OF THINKING

SOUL - CARD THREE REPRESENTS QUALITY OF ENERGY, YOUR INTERNAL DIRECTION AND GUIDANCE FOR THE DAY

PURPORT- as appears or is stated to be true but not necessarily true.

DAILY 3 CARD SPREAD

BODY - CARD ONE REPRESENTS YOUR EXTERNAL REALITY

MIND -CARD TWO REPRESENTS YOUR ATTITUDE, BELIEFS, AND QUALITY OF THINKING

SOUL - CARD THREE REPRESENTS QUALITY OF ENERGY, YOUR INTERNAL DIRECTION AND GUIDANCE FOR THE DAY

PURPORT- as appears or is stated to be true but not necessarily true.

DAILY 3 CARD SPREAD

BODY - CARD ONE REPRESENTS YOUR EXTERNAL REALITY

MIND -CARD TWO REPRESENTS YOUR ATTITUDE, BELIEFS, AND QUALITY OF THINKING

SOUL - CARD THREE REPRESENTS QUALITY OF ENERGY, YOUR INTERNAL DIRECTION AND GUIDANCE FOR THE DAY

PURPORT- as appears or is stated to be true but not necessarily true.

DAILY 3 CARD SPREAD

BODY – CARD ONE REPRESENTS YOUR EXTERNAL REALITY

MIND –CARD TWO REPRESENTS YOUR ATTITUDE, BELIEFS, AND QUALITY OF THINKING

SOUL – CARD THREE REPRESENTS QUALITY OF ENERGY, YOUR INTERNAL DIRECTION AND GUIDANCE FOR THE DAY

PURPORT– as appears or is stated to be true but not necessarily true.

DAILY 3 CARD SPREAD

BODY - CARD ONE REPRESENTS YOUR EXTERNAL REALITY

MIND -CARD TWO REPRESENTS YOUR ATTITUDE, BELIEFS, AND QUALITY OF THINKING

SOUL - CARD THREE REPRESENTS QUALITY OF ENERGY, YOUR INTERNAL DIRECTION AND GUIDANCE FOR THE DAY

PURPORT- as appears or is stated to be true but not necessarily true.

DAILY 3 CARD SPREAD

BODY – CARD ONE REPRESENTS YOUR EXTERNAL REALITY

MIND –CARD TWO REPRESENTS YOUR ATTITUDE, BELIEFS, AND QUALITY OF THINKING

SOUL – CARD THREE REPRESENTS QUALITY OF ENERGY, YOUR INTERNAL DIRECTION AND GUIDANCE FOR THE DAY

PURPORT– as appears or is stated to be true but not necessarily true.

DAILY 3 CARD SPREAD

BODY - CARD ONE REPRESENTS YOUR EXTERNAL REALITY

MIND -CARD TWO REPRESENTS YOUR ATTITUDE, BELIEFS, AND QUALITY OF THINKING

SOUL - CARD THREE REPRESENTS QUALITY OF ENERGY, YOUR INTERNAL DIRECTION AND GUIDANCE FOR THE DAY

PURPORT- as appears or is stated to be true but not necessarily true.

DAILY 3 CARD SPREAD

BODY – CARD ONE REPRESENTS YOUR EXTERNAL REALITY

MIND –CARD TWO REPRESENTS YOUR ATTITUDE, BELIEFS, AND QUALITY OF THINKING

SOUL – CARD THREE REPRESENTS QUALITY OF ENERGY, YOUR INTERNAL DIRECTION AND GUIDANCE FOR THE DAY

PURPORT– as appears or is stated to be true but not necessarily true.

DAILY 3 CARD SPREAD

BODY - CARD ONE REPRESENTS YOUR EXTERNAL REALITY

MIND -CARD TWO REPRESENTS YOUR ATTITUDE, BELIEFS, AND QUALITY OF THINKING

SOUL - CARD THREE REPRESENTS QUALITY OF ENERGY, YOUR INTERNAL DIRECTION AND GUIDANCE FOR THE DAY

PURPORT- as appears or is stated to be true but not necessarily true.

DAILY 3 CARD SPREAD

BODY - CARD ONE REPRESENTS YOUR EXTERNAL REALITY

MIND -CARD TWO REPRESENTS YOUR ATTITUDE, BELIEFS, AND QUALITY OF THINKING

SOUL - CARD THREE REPRESENTS QUALITY OF ENERGY, YOUR INTERNAL DIRECTION AND GUIDANCE FOR THE DAY

PURPORT- as appears or is stated to be true but not necessarily true.

DAILY 3 CARD SPREAD

BODY - CARD ONE REPRESENTS YOUR EXTERNAL REALITY

MIND -CARD TWO REPRESENTS YOUR ATTITUDE, BELIEFS, AND QUALITY OF THINKING

SOUL - CARD THREE REPRESENTS QUALITY OF ENERGY, YOUR INTERNAL DIRECTION AND GUIDANCE FOR THE DAY

PURPORT- as appears or is stated to be true but not necessarily true.

DAILY 3 CARD SPREAD

BODY - CARD ONE REPRESENTS YOUR EXTERNAL REALITY

MIND -CARD TWO REPRESENTS YOUR ATTITUDE, BELIEFS, AND QUALITY OF THINKING

SOUL - CARD THREE REPRESENTS QUALITY OF ENERGY, YOUR INTERNAL DIRECTION AND GUIDANCE FOR THE DAY

PURPORT- as appears or is stated to be true but not necessarily true.

DAILY 3 CARD SPREAD

BODY - CARD ONE REPRESENTS YOUR EXTERNAL REALITY

MIND -CARD TWO REPRESENTS YOUR ATTITUDE, BELIEFS, AND QUALITY OF THINKING

SOUL - CARD THREE REPRESENTS QUALITY OF ENERGY, YOUR INTERNAL DIRECTION AND GUIDANCE FOR THE DAY

PURPORT- as appears or is stated to be true but not necessarily true.

DAILY 3 CARD SPREAD

BODY - CARD ONE REPRESENTS YOUR EXTERNAL REALITY

MIND -CARD TWO REPRESENTS YOUR ATTITUDE, BELIEFS, AND QUALITY OF THINKING

SOUL - CARD THREE REPRESENTS QUALITY OF ENERGY, YOUR INTERNAL DIRECTION AND GUIDANCE FOR THE DAY

PURPORT- as appears or is stated to be true but not necessarily true.

DAILY 3 CARD SPREAD

BODY - CARD ONE REPRESENTS YOUR EXTERNAL REALITY

MIND -CARD TWO REPRESENTS YOUR ATTITUDE, BELIEFS, AND QUALITY OF THINKING

SOUL - CARD THREE REPRESENTS QUALITY OF ENERGY, YOUR INTERNAL DIRECTION AND GUIDANCE FOR THE DAY

PURPORT- as appears or is stated to be true but not necessarily true.

DAILY 3 CARD SPREAD

BODY - CARD ONE REPRESENTS YOUR EXTERNAL REALITY

MIND -CARD TWO REPRESENTS YOUR ATTITUDE, BELIEFS, AND QUALITY OF THINKING

SOUL - CARD THREE REPRESENTS QUALITY OF ENERGY, YOUR INTERNAL DIRECTION AND GUIDANCE FOR THE DAY

PURPORT- as appears or is stated to be true but not necessarily true.

DAILY 3 CARD SPREAD

BODY - CARD ONE REPRESENTS YOUR EXTERNAL REALITY

MIND -CARD TWO REPRESENTS YOUR ATTITUDE, BELIEFS, AND QUALITY OF THINKING

SOUL - CARD THREE REPRESENTS QUALITY OF ENERGY, YOUR INTERNAL DIRECTION AND GUIDANCE FOR THE DAY

PURPORT- as appears or is stated to be true but not necessarily true.

DAILY 3 CARD SPREAD

BODY - CARD ONE REPRESENTS YOUR EXTERNAL REALITY

MIND -CARD TWO REPRESENTS YOUR ATTITUDE, BELIEFS, AND QUALITY OF THINKING

SOUL - CARD THREE REPRESENTS QUALITY OF ENERGY, YOUR INTERNAL DIRECTION AND GUIDANCE FOR THE DAY

PURPORT- as appears or is stated to be true but not necessarily true.

DAILY 3 CARD SPREAD

BODY – CARD ONE REPRESENTS YOUR EXTERNAL REALITY

MIND –CARD TWO REPRESENTS YOUR ATTITUDE, BELIEFS, AND QUALITY OF THINKING

SOUL – CARD THREE REPRESENTS QUALITY OF ENERGY, YOUR INTERNAL DIRECTION AND GUIDANCE FOR THE DAY

PURPORT– as appears or is stated to be true but not necessarily true.

DAILY 3 CARD SPREAD

BODY - CARD ONE REPRESENTS YOUR EXTERNAL REALITY

MIND -CARD TWO REPRESENTS YOUR ATTITUDE, BELIEFS, AND QUALITY OF THINKING

SOUL - CARD THREE REPRESENTS QUALITY OF ENERGY, YOUR INTERNAL DIRECTION AND GUIDANCE FOR THE DAY

PURPORT- as appears or is stated to be true but not necessarily true.

DAILY 3 CARD SPREAD

BODY – CARD ONE REPRESENTS YOUR EXTERNAL REALITY

MIND –CARD TWO REPRESENTS YOUR ATTITUDE, BELIEFS, AND QUALITY OF THINKING

SOUL – CARD THREE REPRESENTS QUALITY OF ENERGY, YOUR INTERNAL DIRECTION AND GUIDANCE FOR THE DAY

PURPORT– as appears or is stated to be true but not necessarily true.

DAILY 3 CARD SPREAD

BODY – CARD ONE REPRESENTS YOUR EXTERNAL REALITY

MIND –CARD TWO REPRESENTS YOUR ATTITUDE, BELIEFS, AND QUALITY OF THINKING

SOUL – CARD THREE REPRESENTS QUALITY OF ENERGY, YOUR INTERNAL DIRECTION AND GUIDANCE FOR THE DAY

PURPORT- as appears or is stated to be true but not necessarily true.

DAILY 3 CARD SPREAD

BODY - CARD ONE REPRESENTS YOUR EXTERNAL REALITY

MIND -CARD TWO REPRESENTS YOUR ATTITUDE, BELIEFS, AND QUALITY OF THINKING

SOUL - CARD THREE REPRESENTS QUALITY OF ENERGY, YOUR INTERNAL DIRECTION AND GUIDANCE FOR THE DAY

PURPORT- as appears or is stated to be true but not necessarily true.

DAILY 3 CARD SPREAD

BODY - CARD ONE REPRESENTS YOUR EXTERNAL REALITY

MIND -CARD TWO REPRESENTS YOUR ATTITUDE, BELIEFS, AND QUALITY OF THINKING

SOUL - CARD THREE REPRESENTS QUALITY OF ENERGY, YOUR INTERNAL DIRECTION AND GUIDANCE FOR THE DAY

PURPORT- as appears or is stated to be true but not necessarily true.

DAILY 3 CARD SPREAD

BODY - CARD ONE REPRESENTS YOUR EXTERNAL REALITY

MIND -CARD TWO REPRESENTS YOUR ATTITUDE, BELIEFS, AND QUALITY OF THINKING

SOUL - CARD THREE REPRESENTS QUALITY OF ENERGY, YOUR INTERNAL DIRECTION AND GUIDANCE FOR THE DAY

PURPORT- as appears or is stated to be true but not necessarily true.

DAILY 3 CARD SPREAD

BODY – CARD ONE REPRESENTS YOUR EXTERNAL REALITY

MIND –CARD TWO REPRESENTS YOUR ATTITUDE, BELIEFS, AND QUALITY OF THINKING

SOUL – CARD THREE REPRESENTS QUALITY OF ENERGY, YOUR INTERNAL DIRECTION AND GUIDANCE FOR THE DAY

PURPORT– as appears or is stated to be true but not necessarily true.

DAILY 3 CARD SPREAD

BODY - CARD ONE REPRESENTS YOUR EXTERNAL REALITY

MIND -CARD TWO REPRESENTS YOUR ATTITUDE, BELIEFS, AND QUALITY OF THINKING

SOUL - CARD THREE REPRESENTS QUALITY OF ENERGY, YOUR INTERNAL DIRECTION AND GUIDANCE FOR THE DAY

PURPORT- as appears or is stated to be true but not necessarily true.

DAILY 3 CARD SPREAD

BODY – CARD ONE REPRESENTS YOUR EXTERNAL REALITY

MIND –CARD TWO REPRESENTS YOUR ATTITUDE, BELIEFS, AND QUALITY OF THINKING

SOUL – CARD THREE REPRESENTS QUALITY OF ENERGY, YOUR INTERNAL DIRECTION AND GUIDANCE FOR THE DAY

PURPORT- as appears or is stated to be true but not necessarily true.

DAILY 3 CARD SPREAD

BODY – CARD ONE REPRESENTS YOUR EXTERNAL REALITY

MIND –CARD TWO REPRESENTS YOUR ATTITUDE, BELIEFS, AND QUALITY OF THINKING

SOUL – CARD THREE REPRESENTS QUALITY OF ENERGY, YOUR INTERNAL DIRECTION AND GUIDANCE FOR THE DAY

PURPORT– as appears or is stated to be true but not necessarily true.

DAILY 3 CARD SPREAD

BODY - CARD ONE REPRESENTS YOUR EXTERNAL REALITY

MIND -CARD TWO REPRESENTS YOUR ATTITUDE, BELIEFS, AND QUALITY OF THINKING

SOUL - CARD THREE REPRESENTS QUALITY OF ENERGY, YOUR INTERNAL DIRECTION AND GUIDANCE FOR THE DAY

PURPORT- as appears or is stated to be true but not necessarily true.

DAILY 3 CARD SPREAD

BODY - CARD ONE REPRESENTS YOUR EXTERNAL REALITY

MIND -CARD TWO REPRESENTS YOUR ATTITUDE, BELIEFS, AND QUALITY OF THINKING

SOUL - CARD THREE REPRESENTS QUALITY OF ENERGY, YOUR INTERNAL DIRECTION AND GUIDANCE FOR THE DAY

PURPORT- as appears or is stated to be true but not necessarily true.

DAILY 3 CARD SPREAD

BODY – CARD ONE REPRESENTS YOUR EXTERNAL REALITY

MIND –CARD TWO REPRESENTS YOUR ATTITUDE, BELIEFS, AND QUALITY OF THINKING

SOUL – CARD THREE REPRESENTS QUALITY OF ENERGY, YOUR INTERNAL DIRECTION AND GUIDANCE FOR THE DAY

PURPORT– as appears or is stated to be true but not necessarily true.

DAILY 3 CARD SPREAD

BODY - CARD ONE REPRESENTS YOUR EXTERNAL REALITY

MIND -CARD TWO REPRESENTS YOUR ATTITUDE, BELIEFS, AND QUALITY OF THINKING

SOUL - CARD THREE REPRESENTS QUALITY OF ENERGY, YOUR INTERNAL DIRECTION AND GUIDANCE FOR THE DAY

PURPORT- as appears or is stated to be true but not necessarily true.

DAILY 3 CARD SPREAD

BODY – CARD ONE REPRESENTS YOUR EXTERNAL REALITY

MIND –CARD TWO REPRESENTS YOUR ATTITUDE, BELIEFS, AND QUALITY OF THINKING

SOUL – CARD THREE REPRESENTS QUALITY OF ENERGY, YOUR INTERNAL DIRECTION AND GUIDANCE FOR THE DAY

PURPORT– as appears or is stated to be true but not necessarily true.

DAILY 3 CARD SPREAD

BODY - CARD ONE REPRESENTS YOUR EXTERNAL REALITY

MIND -CARD TWO REPRESENTS YOUR ATTITUDE, BELIEFS, AND QUALITY OF THINKING

SOUL - CARD THREE REPRESENTS QUALITY OF ENERGY, YOUR INTERNAL DIRECTION AND GUIDANCE FOR THE DAY

PURPORT- as appears or is stated to be true but not necessarily true.

DAILY 3 CARD SPREAD

BODY – CARD ONE REPRESENTS YOUR EXTERNAL REALITY

MIND –CARD TWO REPRESENTS YOUR ATTITUDE, BELIEFS, AND QUALITY OF THINKING

SOUL – CARD THREE REPRESENTS QUALITY OF ENERGY, YOUR INTERNAL DIRECTION AND GUIDANCE FOR THE DAY

PURPORT– as appears or is stated to be true but not necessarily true.

DAILY 3 CARD SPREAD

BODY - CARD ONE REPRESENTS YOUR EXTERNAL REALITY

MIND -CARD TWO REPRESENTS YOUR ATTITUDE, BELIEFS, AND QUALITY OF THINKING

SOUL - CARD THREE REPRESENTS QUALITY OF ENERGY, YOUR INTERNAL DIRECTION AND GUIDANCE FOR THE DAY

PURPORT- as appears or is stated to be true but not necessarily true.

DAILY 3 CARD SPREAD

BODY - CARD ONE REPRESENTS YOUR EXTERNAL REALITY

MIND -CARD TWO REPRESENTS YOUR ATTITUDE, BELIEFS, AND QUALITY OF THINKING

SOUL - CARD THREE REPRESENTS QUALITY OF ENERGY, YOUR INTERNAL DIRECTION AND GUIDANCE FOR THE DAY

PURPORT- as appears or is stated to be true but not necessarily true.

DAILY 3 CARD SPREAD

BODY - CARD ONE REPRESENTS YOUR EXTERNAL REALITY

MIND -CARD TWO REPRESENTS YOUR ATTITUDE, BELIEFS, AND QUALITY OF THINKING

SOUL - CARD THREE REPRESENTS QUALITY OF ENERGY, YOUR INTERNAL DIRECTION AND GUIDANCE FOR THE DAY

PURPORT- as appears or is stated to be true but not necessarily true.

DAILY 3 CARD SPREAD

BODY - CARD ONE REPRESENTS YOUR EXTERNAL REALITY

MIND -CARD TWO REPRESENTS YOUR ATTITUDE, BELIEFS, AND QUALITY OF THINKING

SOUL - CARD THREE REPRESENTS QUALITY OF ENERGY, YOUR INTERNAL DIRECTION AND GUIDANCE FOR THE DAY

PURPORT- as appears or is stated to be true but not necessarily true.

DAILY 3 CARD SPREAD

BODY - CARD ONE REPRESENTS YOUR EXTERNAL REALITY

MIND -CARD TWO REPRESENTS YOUR ATTITUDE, BELIEFS, AND QUALITY OF THINKING

SOUL - CARD THREE REPRESENTS QUALITY OF ENERGY, YOUR INTERNAL DIRECTION AND GUIDANCE FOR THE DAY

PURPORT- as appears or is stated to be true but not necessarily true.

DAILY 3 CARD SPREAD

BODY - CARD ONE REPRESENTS YOUR EXTERNAL REALITY

MIND -CARD TWO REPRESENTS YOUR ATTITUDE, BELIEFS, AND QUALITY OF THINKING

SOUL - CARD THREE REPRESENTS QUALITY OF ENERGY, YOUR INTERNAL DIRECTION AND GUIDANCE FOR THE DAY

PURPORT- as appears or is stated to be true but not necessarily true.

DAILY 3 CARD SPREAD

BODY - CARD ONE REPRESENTS YOUR EXTERNAL REALITY

MIND -CARD TWO REPRESENTS YOUR ATTITUDE, BELIEFS, AND QUALITY OF THINKING

SOUL - CARD THREE REPRESENTS QUALITY OF ENERGY, YOUR INTERNAL DIRECTION AND GUIDANCE FOR THE DAY

PURPORT- as appears or is stated to be true but not necessarily true.

DAILY 3 CARD SPREAD

BODY – CARD ONE REPRESENTS YOUR EXTERNAL REALITY

MIND –CARD TWO REPRESENTS YOUR ATTITUDE, BELIEFS, AND QUALITY OF THINKING

SOUL – CARD THREE REPRESENTS QUALITY OF ENERGY, YOUR INTERNAL DIRECTION AND GUIDANCE FOR THE DAY

PURPORT– as appears or is stated to be true but not necessarily true.

DAILY 3 CARD SPREAD

BODY - CARD ONE REPRESENTS YOUR EXTERNAL REALITY

MIND -CARD TWO REPRESENTS YOUR ATTITUDE, BELIEFS, AND QUALITY OF THINKING

SOUL - CARD THREE REPRESENTS QUALITY OF ENERGY, YOUR INTERNAL DIRECTION AND GUIDANCE FOR THE DAY

PURPORT- as appears or is stated to be true but not necessarily true.

DAILY 3 CARD SPREAD

BODY - CARD ONE REPRESENTS YOUR EXTERNAL REALITY

MIND -CARD TWO REPRESENTS YOUR ATTITUDE, BELIEFS, AND QUALITY OF THINKING

SOUL - CARD THREE REPRESENTS QUALITY OF ENERGY, YOUR INTERNAL DIRECTION AND GUIDANCE FOR THE DAY

PURPORT- as appears or is stated to be true but not necessarily true.

DAILY 3 CARD SPREAD

BODY - CARD ONE REPRESENTS YOUR EXTERNAL REALITY

MIND -CARD TWO REPRESENTS YOUR ATTITUDE, BELIEFS, AND QUALITY OF THINKING

SOUL - CARD THREE REPRESENTS QUALITY OF ENERGY, YOUR INTERNAL DIRECTION AND GUIDANCE FOR THE DAY

PURPORT- as appears or is stated to be true but not necessarily true.

DAILY 3 CARD SPREAD

BODY - CARD ONE REPRESENTS YOUR EXTERNAL REALITY

MIND -CARD TWO REPRESENTS YOUR ATTITUDE, BELIEFS, AND QUALITY OF THINKING

SOUL - CARD THREE REPRESENTS QUALITY OF ENERGY, YOUR INTERNAL DIRECTION AND GUIDANCE FOR THE DAY

PURPORT- as appears or is stated to be true but not necessarily true.

DAILY 3 CARD SPREAD

BODY - CARD ONE REPRESENTS YOUR EXTERNAL REALITY

MIND -CARD TWO REPRESENTS YOUR ATTITUDE, BELIEFS, AND QUALITY OF THINKING

SOUL - CARD THREE REPRESENTS QUALITY OF ENERGY, YOUR INTERNAL DIRECTION AND GUIDANCE FOR THE DAY

PURPORT- as appears or is stated to be true but not necessarily true.

DAILY 3 CARD SPREAD

BODY - CARD ONE REPRESENTS YOUR EXTERNAL REALITY

MIND - CARD TWO REPRESENTS YOUR ATTITUDE, BELIEFS, AND QUALITY OF THINKING

SOUL - CARD THREE REPRESENTS QUALITY OF ENERGY, YOUR INTERNAL DIRECTION AND GUIDANCE FOR THE DAY

PURPORT- as appears or is stated to be true but not necessarily true.

DAILY 3 CARD SPREAD

BODY - CARD ONE REPRESENTS YOUR EXTERNAL REALITY

MIND -CARD TWO REPRESENTS YOUR ATTITUDE, BELIEFS, AND QUALITY OF THINKING

SOUL - CARD THREE REPRESENTS QUALITY OF ENERGY, YOUR INTERNAL DIRECTION AND GUIDANCE FOR THE DAY

PURPORT- as appears or is stated to be true but not necessarily true.

DAILY 3 CARD SPREAD

BODY – CARD ONE REPRESENTS YOUR EXTERNAL REALITY

MIND –CARD TWO REPRESENTS YOUR ATTITUDE, BELIEFS, AND QUALITY OF THINKING

SOUL – CARD THREE REPRESENTS QUALITY OF ENERGY, YOUR INTERNAL DIRECTION AND GUIDANCE FOR THE DAY

PURPORT– as appears or is stated to be true but not necessarily true.

DAILY 3 CARD SPREAD

BODY - CARD ONE REPRESENTS YOUR EXTERNAL REALITY

MIND -CARD TWO REPRESENTS YOUR ATTITUDE, BELIEFS, AND QUALITY OF THINKING

SOUL - CARD THREE REPRESENTS QUALITY OF ENERGY, YOUR INTERNAL DIRECTION AND GUIDANCE FOR THE DAY

PURPORT- as appears or is stated to be true but not necessarily true.

DAILY 3 CARD SPREAD

BODY – CARD ONE REPRESENTS YOUR EXTERNAL REALITY

MIND –CARD TWO REPRESENTS YOUR ATTITUDE, BELIEFS, AND QUALITY OF THINKING

SOUL – CARD THREE REPRESENTS QUALITY OF ENERGY, YOUR INTERNAL DIRECTION AND GUIDANCE FOR THE DAY

PURPORT– as appears or is stated to be true but not necessarily true.

TAROT READING PREDICTIONS

Asking when something will happen in a reading is done with Zodiac Signs in cards to be read as the time frame.

Zodiac signs on Tarot Cards:

Aries corresponds the Emperor Card– March 21 – April 20

Taurus corresponds to Hierophant Card – April 21 – May 20

Gemini corresponds to Lovers Card – May 22 – June 21

Cancer corresponds to The Chariot Card – June 22 – July 23

Leo corresponds to The Strength Card – July 23 – August 23

Virgo corresponds to The Hermit Card – August 24 –September 22

Libra corresponds to Justice & Adjustment Card
– September 23 – October 23

Scorpio corresponds to The Death Card –
October 24 – November 22

Sagittarius corresponds to The Temperance
Card – November 23 – December 22

Capricorn corresponds to The Devil Card –
December 22 – January 20

Aquarius corresponds to The Star Card – January
21 – February 18

Pisces corresponds to The Moon Card –
February 19– March 20

Days of the Week Correspondences

Sunday	The Sun Card	Sun
Monday Moon	High Priestess Card	
Tuesday	Tower Card	Mars
Wednesday Mercury	Magician	
Thursday Jupiter	Wheel of Fortune	
Friday	Empress Card	Venus
Saturday	World Card	Saturn

Printed in Great Britain
by Amazon